SCARED TO DEATH

SCARED TO DEATH

A JUNIPER GROVE MYSTERY

KARIN KAUFMAN

CHAPTER 1

The interior of the Grandview Hotel was quite possibly the dreariest thing I'd ever seen. And I was destined to stay there overnight. My friend Holly Kavanagh had been offered the chance of a lifetime by the millionaire owner of the hotel—catering a gathering there—and I had agreed to go along for moral support. So had Julia Foster, our sixty-something neighbor on Finch Hill Road. By the looks of the lobby, Holly was going to need every ounce of support we could muster.

The Grandview was privately owned, but not so the five acres of land it sat on. Though the hotel was set in the Colorado foothills four miles northwest of Juniper Grove proper, the land belonged to the town. The Grandview had been built in 1908, back when luxury and chunkiness were synonymous. Ornate coffered ceilings, dark wood paneling, massive interior columns. I figured the decor was appropriate for a hotel whose claim to fame was a mysterious and unsolved murder in room 108. Seriously, people paid extra to stay in that room. And gangster Al Capone had used the hotel as a hideaway, staying in a less popular room on the third floor.

The three of us stood in the empty lobby, our suitcases at our feet. Holly was chewing on the inside of her lower lip and fiddling with her wedding ring, probably reconsidering her decision to stay at the hotel. She'd left her husband, Peter, in charge of her bakery—and of Caleb, their thirteen-year-old son—to serve pastries to a talk-radio host and his assistants before, during, and after their live broadcast from room 108.

"Tell me again why I agreed to do this," she said.

"Because Arthur Jago loves your baking and is going to help you expand Holly's Sweets," I replied.

Julia gave a mock shiver. "Now tell me why *I* agreed to this."

Holly elbowed Julia. "You agreed because we're friends and you didn't want me to be alone in this creepy place."

"And Peter, sensible man that he is, wouldn't let you go alone," Julia said.

"Now that we have that straight." I snapped up my small suitcase. "Come on, you two, we can do this. It's just a hotel." I strode to the receptionist's desk and dinged the call bell.

Moments after I heard the echo of footsteps down a distant hall, a tall, potbellied man in a bold plaid sweater rounded a corner into the lobby, his eyes settling on Holly. He broke into a broad smile. "I'm so glad you could make it," he said, giving her a quick, restrained hug. His was a round, Humpty Dumpty kind of face, with a hairline that had receded a good two inches, a neatly trimmed gray beard, and a small, pink mouth. A friendly face, I thought. Not that my record on judging faces was anything to crow about. It was dismal, in fact.

"Arthur," Holly said. "Thank you for inviting me."

"No, thank *you* for coming out here on a cold January

evening. I know this isn't your cup of tea, but if Shane Rooney goes crazy over your pastries on live radio tonight, and he will, that alone will be worth your while. His station's signal reaches north to Wyoming and south to Denver." He rubbed his hands together. "And where are those lovely pastries of yours? And by pastries, I mean eclairs. You know how I love them."

"In my SUV at the side of the building," Holly said, digging her keys from her coat pocket. "We need to go back."

"You stay right there." He reached out and slapped the bell. "I closed the hotel to guests for the event, but the managers are still here. And you can leave your car parked where it is."

Holly gestured toward me and Julia. "These are the friends I told you about. Rachel Stowe and Julia Foster."

"Welcome ladies," Arthur said, shaking first Julia's hand and then mine. "Are you ready? You're in for an experience tonight."

"That's what I'm afraid of," Julia said.

"Don't you worry. You'll have the time of your life." Just as Arthur raised his hand to ring the bell again, a large carved door on the other side of the lobby swung open and a man and woman hastened to the receptionist's desk.

"Let me introduce Ian and Connie Swanson," Arthur said. "Managers of the Grandview for three years now. They have a suite on the third floor."

"So if you need anything at all, any time of night, don't hesitate," Ian said, stepping forward to grasp Holly's hand.

Another round of handshaking and introductions ensued, after which Arthur asked the Swansons to retrieve the pastries from Holly's car and take them to the kitchen.

Connie nodded eagerly, telling Holly what a fan she was of her bakery, then took her keys and marched for the door, Ian on her heels.

"It's snowing," Holly called out.

"We're fine," Ian yelled over his shoulder.

Wearing only sweaters and jeans, the two headed out into the brewing storm.

"They're young," Arthur said. "They can handle a little cold."

The Swansons weren't *that* young. Early forties, probably. But I could tell they were keen on pleasing Arthur—without delay.

On the other hand, at forty-three, and wearing my warmest winter coat, I was about to tell Arthur to turn up the heat in his drafty hotel lobby. Cold air seeped around the window cases—I felt it at the back of my neck—and poured under the front door, scuttling across the lobby on its way to my legs. I hoped our rooms on the first floor were a good ten degrees warmer, but I had my doubts. Even a millionaire had limits on how much he'd spend to heat a windy old hotel during the coldest month of the year.

"The Swansons will take care of beverages and sandwiches," Arthur said, "and the rest is up to you, Holly."

"And there are still ten altogether?" Holly said. "Have I got that right?"

"Me, your friends, and the Swansons included, yes," Arthur said. "The radio folks are back in the room, setting up for the broadcast." He tossed his head toward the hall. "You'll meet that ravenous bunch in a minute. Why don't I show you ladies to your rooms?"

He plucked large, old-fashioned keys from hooks behind the front desk, and we followed him down the same hall he'd taken to the lobby, me carrying my tiny case and Julia and Holly wheeling their suitcases behind them.

"Holly, you're in 105," Arthur said. "Rachel, I've got you in 106, and Julia, you're in 107."

Julia shot furtive looks at the closed door of room 108. "It's just across the hall," she said, tugging at one of the curls in her gray hair.

"Yes, that's the very room," Arthur said proudly. "Fifty years ago tonight, Herbert Purdy died in room 108, behind a locked door. I was all of twelve years old and living in Denver at the time, but I heard about it. His murder was never solved—it was *impossible* to solve—and Purdy is said to roam the halls, especially on the anniversary of his death, looking for justice."

Arthur no doubt thought he was supplying us with charmingly spooky commentary, but the more he talked, the paler Julia looked. I discreetly elbowed Holly.

"Would it be all right with you if Julia and I exchanged rooms?" she asked Arthur.

The furrows in Julia's brow relaxed ever so slightly.

"Oh, sure, sleep in any of the three you want," he said, handing Holly all three keys. "The rooms on the second and third floors are closed to guests until next week, unfortunately."

"Can I see the Al Capone room later?" I asked.

"Your sure can, Rachel," Arthur said. "It's unlocked, so you head on up there whenever you want. Room 312 in the southwest corner of the building. Three of Capone's men were across the hall in 311. I hear they wanted an unobstructed view of the only decent approaches to the hotel back then. It's less isolated now, of course, but this used to be a hideaway. Well, ladies," he added with a slight bow,

"I'll leave you to it. Get settled and join us in room 108. Holly, I'm sure your pastries are safe in the kitchen by now."

Arthur trudged off down the hall, the palms of his large hands facing backward and his long arms slicing the air as though he were propelling himself through water.

Holly gave us our keys, and we entered our separate rooms. Julia let out a grunt that traveled up the hall. If her room was anything like mine, I knew why. The hotel's dark and heavy decor, historical though it may have been, had foolishly been carried out in the rooms. *Unpleasant* was the first, and kindest, word that came to mind. A rustle at my door made me turn.

"I see yours is the same," Julia said, looking as though she'd just taken a bite of a particularly vinegary pickle.

"I don't understand it," I said, laying my suitcase on the bed. "Some fresh paint and new bedding could make this a lovely hotel. Arthur can't be making that much money from its dilapidated reputation."

Julia wandered into the room, her eyes searching for a place to sit. She passed by a scruffy oval-backed armchair near the door in favor of my bed. "I wonder if the radio station is paying to use that room."

"Maybe." I unzipped my suitcase. "Or maybe Arthur isn't charging them because he figures the publicity is pay enough." I hung my extra sweater and pair of jeans in the room's tiny armoire and emptied the plastic bags carrying my toiletries onto a miniature vanity in the miniature bathroom. "But don't you think it's odd that Arthur closed the hotel to paying guests on his biggest night of the year? Julia?"

My friend was staring ahead, her eyes unfocused as if she were lost in thought. My unpacking done, I sat next to her.

"I was just thinking, Rachel," she said. "What were you saying?"

"This place is really bothering you, isn't it?"

"No, no," she said, shooing my words away. "I can't shake this bad feeling, but honest to goodness, who wouldn't feel bad in a hotel like this? It's designed to make you feel bad. That's what people pay for, isn't it? I'll be fine."

"If you want to go home, I can take Holly's car and drive you."

"On those roads? With that storm picking up?" She forced a smile. "I'm not going anywhere until morning."

"Let's go see what Holly's room looks like." I rose, tugged at Julia's cardigan, and walked next door, where I found Holly talking with Connie Swanson about the serving schedule, which I immediately gathered didn't exist. Holly was to present her pastries, simple as that, and the hungry radio host and his tech support would devour them until they were gone.

"Bring them in two waves, I think," Connie said, flicking back strands of brown hair. "That way we can make room by clearing the empty trays from the first wave."

"Sounds good," Holly said. "Better than continually carrying in the food."

"How are your rooms, ladies?" Connie said, turning her attention to Julia and me.

"As expected," Julia said.

Connie chuckled. "I hope that's good, but I fear it's not."

"Well, it's just a little . . ."

"Dark?" Connie suggested. "Ian and I are making headway convincing Arthur to upgrade, but we're not there yet. At the moment we're doing a little too much business with the ghost crowd. We had twenty Japanese guests last month—all but one of them here because of Herbert Purdy. The other was here for Al Capone. Six of them claimed they saw a ghost, so guess what? We have two dozen more coming from Japan next week. And a TV show wants to book us in February."

"I've read a little about the Purdy murder," Holly said, "but I don't understand why people are fixated on it."

"Well, let me tell you about Herbert Purdy." Connie sat on the edge of the armchair by Holly's door and launched into what I was sure was a well-rehearsed account. "He was a fifty-two-year-old businessman on his way from Sterling, Colorado to Craig, up in the mountains. His family was there on winter vacation, waiting for him, so he planned a one-night stay at the Grandview. All the hotel guests testified that Purdy seemed happy and relaxed that night. He ate dinner, talked to other travelers, and went to bed about ten o'clock. When he didn't show up at checkout time the next morning, a maid knocked on his door. The manager had to open the door, and when he did, there Purdy was. In his pajamas, flat on his stomach in bed, a knife in his back. Your classic locked-room mystery."

CHAPTER 2

I cleared my throat. "It's not really a locked-room mystery," I said, breaking the spell Connie wanted to weave. "The staff must have had access to Purdy's room, and if the keys back then were hung in the lobby like they are now, so did everyone else. The killer had a key. He killed Purdy, went out to the hall, and then locked the door with the key."

Connie bit her lip, squelching a grin. "Whatever you do, don't tell Shane Rooney that. He lives for the locked-room aspect of it all. He talks about the Purdy murder every January on his radio show, hoping his audience won't point out the glaring hole in his logic."

"So you know it wasn't a locked-room murder?" Holly said, dropping to her bed.

"It was just an ordinary, straightforward murder," she replied.

"I don't know about straightforward," I said. "Who would murder a stranger in an isolated hotel? Two enemies just happen to meet in the Colorado foothills in January? It's not likely. Plus, Purdy was stabbed in the back while he was wearing his pajamas. He must have let the killer in, maybe after he'd gone to bed. It's pretty weird, if you ask me."

"Okay, now *that's* what you say to Rooney," Connie said with a laugh. "He'll love you for it." She stood and smoothed her black skirt. "Why don't I introduce you to him and his crew? Arthur's already in there." Just outside Holly's door, she paused and turned back. "I almost forgot. If you hear banging noises tonight, don't worry. We're not sure what it is, but we think it's the air ducts contracting. They're so old, they probably need to be replaced."

Julia's eyes widened, but she gamely followed us to meet the radio crew. I wondered seriously if she was going to make it through the night or if I'd have to make a midnight trip out of the foothills in Holly's car.

Room 108 was a hive of activity. Connie pointed out Shane Rooney—a tall, blond-haired man—and his three assistants before leaving with Holly to rustle up the crew's pastries, but Julia and I remained just outside the door, trying to stay out of the way. Two of Rooney's crew were hooking up various pieces of equipment—some of which I suspected had more to do with ghosts than with broadcasting—and the third was talking with Rooney over a computer on the room's desk.

Arthur Jago, looking like a proud papa on the verge of handing out cigars, was perched on the room's substantial windowsill and was watching the proceedings while gobbling one of Holly's eclairs.

"Air ducts, my foot," Julia whispered.

"Don't think about it," I whispered back. "What's that satellite-looking thing by the window?"

One of the crew wheeled back to me. His hands stuffed in his jeans pockets, he smiled broadly, showing me his large and perfectly spaced teeth. "That's an antenna, which is hooked up to our transmitter," he said.

"You have good hearing," I said. "I'm Rachel Stowe and this is my friend Julia Foster."

He took two long strides toward the door, stepping over cables and surge protectors, and greeted us with a handshake. In his mid-thirties, he was good looking in a male model kind of way. His brown hair was cut in one of those short but high-rise styles that I imagined took a mountain of gel to maintain and collapsed at the first sign of humidity. "It pays to have good hearing in radio," he said. "I'm Dustin Littlefield, the engineer. We go live in forty-five minutes. Staying?"

"If we can squeeze in here," I replied. The room was sparsely furnished, and the only places to sit, aside from the windowsill, were at the desk or on the rumpled bed.

Dustin smiled again and rocked back on his heels. "I think we can get you in. But you have to *shhh*." He held a finger to his lips.

"We'll be so quiet you won't know we're here," Julia promised, visions of abandonment to the dark halls of Grandview while the radio crew sat in warmth and light preying on her mind, I was sure.

I pulled my eyes from the bed. Surely that wasn't *the* bed? The hotel must have replaced it since Purdy's murder. "How long is the show tonight?" I asked.

"Four hours," Dustin said. "Normally Shane broadcasts for three, but we allotted an extra hour for the ghost to show up. Spirits are seldom punctual. It's rude of them, but what can you do?"

"I guess they don't have to be punctual anymore," I said. "They can't be fired."

Julia smiled wanly, playing the good sport as best she could. I had never known my neighbor to be anything less than level-headed—even hard-nosed—when it came to what she called superstition, but this evening she was on edge.

15

Connie's remark about the air ducts hadn't helped.

When Dustin returned to his work, I leaned close to her, keeping my voice low. "You know this is hype for a radio show, don't you? If they hear the ductwork contracting, they'll say Purdy is roaming the halls."

"I'd better not hear the ducts. Or creaking floorboards or anything else."

"This is an old place, Julia. You're sure to hear things."

"Thank you very much. I'm *so* looking forward to this."

I heard a soft clinking sound and turned to see Holly, Connie, and Ian making their way toward us, each bearing an overstuffed tray—Holly's and Connie's brimming with pastries and Ian's weighted down with two full coffeepots and a dozen cups.

"Holly brought your favorite raspberry scones," I said, hoping to distract Julia from thoughts of ghostly apparitions. "Let's get scones and cream puffs before everything disappears."

Before Holly could maneuver her way into the room, Julia grabbed a scone and I snatched napkins and a cream puff from her tray.

"I brought extra cream puffs in my suitcase," Holly said.

"I knew I liked you," I said with a grin.

As quickly as they entered, Connie and Ian exited the crowded room, excusing themselves and inviting those who wanted more coffee to seek out the kitchen on the other side of the hotel. There were murmurs of appreciation from around the room as Shane, Dustin, and the others dove into the trays, ignoring the coffee in favor of the pastries.

"It's like watching a pack of coyotes," Julia said.

16

"Hungry, hard-working coyotes," Shane said, sidestepping to the door.

It was becoming clear that however quietly Julia and I spoke, we were bound to be overheard. Either the acoustics in the room and hall were fantastic or people in the radio business had exceptional hearing.

"I'd shake your hands, but mine are covered in powdered sugar," he added. "I heard Holly say your names a few minutes ago. Rachel and Julia?"

"Yup," I said. "And you're Shane Rooney?"

"Guilty as charged. Are we ready for some spooky fun tonight?"

"No," Julia said flatly. "I certainly am not."

"Oh, come on now," he said. "I promise you'll have a good time. You stick with me and you'll be fine. No worries. It's going to be a blast." He chuckled gently as he spoke, turning the donut over in his hand as though trying to decide where to bite next. He was about my age—younger than I'd imagined a veteran radio host to be—with dark brown eyes, an athletic build, and short, curly hair.

"A long time ago I saw a horror movie that started just like this," Julia said.

Shane let out a belly laugh, and to my relief, Julia cracked a smile. Her first since we'd arrived at the Grandview. But just as she opened her mouth to speak, he threw his hand in the air and called for quiet. His crew froze, and Shane stood with his head tilted, listening.

A moment later, I heard it too. A distant clanging sound.

"Conyer, Maria, go get that," Dustin ordered. "The basement door is at the other end of the hall on the left."

Conyer, a red-haired young man sporting round wire-

17

rimmed glasses, set off immediately, taking a microphone and recorder with him, but Maria, a short, slight woman in her early thirties, didn't budge.

"Gimme a flashlight," she said, her hand out, waiting. "I'm not going anywhere without one."

"You're a wise woman, Miss Hall," Shane said.

Dustin handed her a flashlight and told her to hurry before the noise stopped. "I want recordings," he called as she darted out the door.

"What *is* that?" Holly said.

"Air ducts contracting?" Arthur said, sounding rather unsure. "Connie said when they turn the heat down, the ducts start banging."

Turn the heat down? I thought. *Isn't it already down?* I was going to need a blanket in a minute.

"That doesn't sound like contracting ducts to me," Holly said. "It's too rhythmic and constant. Ducts bang once and then you don't hear anything for awhile. I assume there's a basement?"

"Sure is," Arthur said.

"Let's just say it's the ducts and be done with it," Julia said, her eyes riveted to the floor.

Shane let out another laugh, but this time Julia didn't join in.

"I challenge you to find a building this old that doesn't make strange noises," I said, more for Julia's benefit than Holly's.

"Are you a skeptic, Rachel?" Shane asked.

"Only about some things," I answered. "Can I have half a cheese Danish, Holly?" Maybe the sight of me indulging in too many pastries would take Julia's mind and ears off the banging sound. Since I'd started dating James

Gilroy, Juniper Grove's police chief, her comments about my eating habits had grown more vociferous. Not that I was about to change. I loved my cream puffs, and that was that. Besides—and this was quite astonishing—James Gilroy liked me just the way I was.

But even as Holly sliced a Danish in two and handed me half, Julia continued to stare at the floor, struggling to identify the noise and paying scant attention to everything else around her.

"How long have we got?" Shane said.

"What do you mean how long have we got?" Julia said, clutching her breastbone.

"The show, Miss Julia," Shane said with a wink. "Nothing more deadly than that."

"Half an hour," Dustin said.

"Is it all right with you if I go listen, Arthur?" Shane said. "Recordings don't do it for me. I want to find this noise and talk to it in person." He popped the rest of his donut in his mouth and wiped his hands on his jeans.

"Be my guest," Arthur said.

With that, the rest of the crew took off, leaving a smiling Arthur to contemplate the pastry trays.

"Do you mind if we go too?" I asked.

Julia was aghast. "I'm not going anywhere," she declared. "I'm not stepping foot outside this room."

I was thinking of history, not ghosts. I had a feeling Al Capone's men, and some of his bootleg liquor, had been in that basement, and I wanted to see for myself. But I had another purpose in mind, too. If Holly and I discovered a humdrum, ordinary source of that noise, we could put Julia's mind at rest.

"You stay here with me, Mrs. Foster," Arthur said.

"Let me pour you a steaming cup of coffee."

While Julia watched us, mystified by our need to see the basement, Holly and I dug up a flashlight and headed out of the room.

CHAPTER 3

A bare lightbulb hanging above the landing lit the wooden stairs leading down to the basement. Just barely. Near the bottom of the stairs, I flicked on our flashlight and swept the beam over the floor and walls. The foundation and walls were constructed of thick stone, and the floor, such as it was, was dirt. The air smelled of mold and mildew, and I was sure I heard mice scurrying along the walls, but the banging sound had ceased.

"Where did everyone go?" I whispered, creeping forward.

"I don't hear them," Holly whispered back. "They couldn't have gone far." She grasped her long, dark ponytail, pulled it over her shoulder, and hung onto it as though it were a lifeline.

"Why are we whispering?"

"I don't know."

"I hear someone moving."

"So do I."

I halted and turned off my flashlight.

"For goodness' sakes, don't do that," Holly said.

"Look over there," I said, pointing ahead to the beam from another flashlight. "Who's here?" I called out.

"It's just me, Maria Hall," a woman's voice called

back. "I'll keep talking and you keep walking toward my voice. It's like a smelly maze down here. I can't even tell how big it is. I think I've been walking in circles."

As we started forward, I turned on my flashlight and scanned the floor, certain I was about to trip over an old barrel of bootleg whiskey or a nest of mice. The dust and mold tickled my nose, and I was considering turning back when we finally found Maria, the woman who had demanded her own flashlight before venturing downstairs. Standing in the center of a partially walled-off section of the basement, she directed her flashlight in my eyes and then quickly lowered it.

"I'm glad to see real flesh-and-blood human beings," she said. "Everyone disappeared. I can't hear them, can you? It's as if they left already. And it stinks like an old gym sock down here." She laughed, but the anxiety in her voice was almost palpable.

"I don't hear the banging sound," I said. "When did it stop?"

"The last time I heard it was at the top of the stairs," Maria said. "I've been trying to find out where that light is coming from. See it over there?"

When Maria cast her flashlight behind her, I noticed a slight tremor in her hand, and when her other hand rose to her face, her fingers quivered slightly as she brushed the headband holding back her dark hair.

"It must be a ceiling fixture," I said. "The light looks stationary. How about going back upstairs?"

"Conyer has the recorder," she said. "I need to make sure he got something before I go back up or Shane will kill me."

"Listen," Holly said, grasping my arm.

Suddenly I heard the clanging noise again, only more distant this time. "It doesn't seem to be coming from the basement. Or at least not this part of the basement." I directed my light at the ceiling and found a long line of ductwork running the length of the room before angling around the corner. "There isn't any noise coming from *this* duct, and if it was coming from another duct, wouldn't it echo through all the ducts?"

"Who's doing that?" Maria said, anger working its way into her voice. "Someone's messing around with us."

"Quiet you two," Holly said, still holding my arm. "Something's moving."

I pointed my flashlight in the direction of the stationary light and strained to listen.

When Shane emerged from around the corner, his finger to his lips, I nearly jumped out of my skin.

Maria smacked him on his shoulder. "Stop it! I'm not getting paid enough for this, and it isn't funny."

"I'm not trying to be funny," he said. "Do you hear that banging sound again?"

We all nodded.

"No way, José, is that an air duct," he said. "But whatever it is, you can't tell where it's coming from. It could be coming from the basement or from up above. Maybe pipes or plumbing vents are carrying the noise from one of the floors. You know, the way you can hear bathroom water running two stories above you in an apartment building."

Maria turned slowly in place, her flashlight beam arcing over the walls like the revolving beacon in a lighthouse. She was a thin woman, a couple inches shorter than my five foot seven, and her stature must have made her feel vulnerable, adding to her fear. "We have to start the show," she said, her voice soft and quavering. "We're cutting this too close and the station's going to have our heads."

"Where is everybody?" Shane said.

"Probably upstairs, eating all the donuts," Holly answered. "We'd better get ours before it's too late." She'd sensed Maria's growing panic, I realized, and wanted to give her a face-saving way of making a rapid exit.

"I'm going to open the show talking about that sound and how we hunted for it," Shane said. "Bring the audience in on the real sights and sounds of the Grandview."

"Goody," Maria said.

"You heard it, Maria," Shane said. "Same as I did."

"I hate this," Maria said.

I took the lead heading back to the stairs, and Shane, whose curiosity appeared to overwhelm any fear he might have felt, brought up the rear. Two minutes later we were back in room 108, much to the relief of a nerve-wracked Julia.

"Where have you been? And where's Arthur?" she said.

"I don't know," I said, looking about the room as if I might come upon the very large Arthur Jago hiding in such a small place. Dustin and Conyer had returned and were already at work, preparing to go on the air, and Shane and Maria had pushed past me into the room, both of them heading for the computer. "Where *is* Arthur? I thought he was staying here with you."

"He poured me a cup of coffee, said he had to go somewhere important, and that's the last I saw of him," Julia said. "I was sitting here by myself until Dustin and Conyer showed up." She leaned close and lowered her voice.

"Conyer's had three cinnamon-honey rolls just since I've been here. I don't know where he's putting it, but I expect his stomach to burst at any moment. We may have to clear the room."

"Arthur sounded like he intended to wait with you until we got back," Holly said.

"Well, he didn't," Julia said. "What if the lights had gone out? Didn't I say this would happen? Sitting here listening to that clanging all by myself, wondering who might be creeping down the hall, coming toward this room."

"Quiet, please," Dustin called, his forefinger in the air. "Five seconds." At the count of five, he pointed at Shane.

"Good evening, listeners, and welcome to this special edition of the Shane Rooney Show," Shane said. "We're coming to you live from the Grandview Hotel on the fiftieth anniversary of the mysterious and unsolved murder of Herbert Purdy. Fifty years ago tonight, a traveler on his way to the mountains met his untimely death. Some say Purdy still walks the halls of the Grandview. Does he? I can tell you this much. Moments ago, my crew and I heard unidentified sounds coming from the dark basement of this hotel." He paused, letting his audience savor that juicy bit of news.

In that moment of silence, a shriek cut through the air.

Shane jumped in his seat, and Maria jerked and spun toward the sound.

"What on earth?" Dustin said, irritated by the interruption.

When another shriek sounded, Julia dug her fingers into my arm.

"Where is that coming from?" Conyer said, pushing his glasses up his nose.

"Sorry for the unintended broadcast break, folks," Shane said into the microphone. "But how's that for atmosphere? Were you able to hear that? A scream in the night. We'll be right back." He pushed a button on his microphone and rushed for the door, steps ahead of everyone else in the room.

It took only seconds to find the source of the screams. At the far end of the hall, a shaking Connie Swanson was standing with her hands to her mouth. "He's in the library," she said, her voice now reduced to a raspy whisper.

At first I saw nothing but chairs and bookshelves. Shane and Dustin maneuvered around me into the library, and I followed. A moment later we were all staring at a very still and obviously dead Arthur Jago in a high-backed armchair, an open book across his legs, a look of terror etched on his face. When Shane touched him, he slumped forward.

"That's a knife in his back," Holly said. "Someone stabbed him."

A wood-handled knife protruded from the middle of his upper back. I turned, put a hand on Holly's shoulder, and then shot a look at Julia in the hall, warning her to stay out.

"Connie! Where are you?"

Ian Swanson called out again, and I saw him outside the door, dashing to his wife's side. "What is it? What's wrong?"

"He's dead, Ian. Arthur is dead."

Ian stared at his wife as though he had trouble comprehending her simple words. "Did he have a heart attack?"

"Someone killed him," Connie breathed, her voice again no more than a whisper. "Stabbed him. That's the

26

kitchen knife we were looking for."

Ian walked slowly into the room, his eyes shooting from Shane to Dustin and finally to the armchair. He gasped.

Shane glanced at his wristwatch and raked his fingers through his hair. "All right, now. Someone call the police or sheriff—whichever it is out here."

"Police," I said. "Technically, we're in Juniper Grove."

"Right, then," Shane said. "The commercials are almost over. I have to get back on the air."

"You can't do that," Maria said from the doorway.

"I can't leave dead air," Shane said.

"He's right," Dustin said. "I'm going back to the console."

"Are you kidding me?" Maria said, gaping as Shane and Dustin raced off. "What are you going to say?" she shouted.

Ian retreated to the hallway, but Holly and I lingered in the library. My eyes roamed the room, searching for clues, trying to memorize every detail. There was something more than a little odd about the scene before me, starting with the book on Arthur's lap. I glanced up. "Has anyone called the police?"

"I will right now," Ian said. He took his wife's hand and pulled her away from the door. "Let's go to the front desk, Connie."

"I'm going back to the show," Maria said. "I don't have a choice." She slunk away, seemingly embarrassed by the necessary deference to her job.

I waited for the sound of Maria's footsteps to fade and then turned to Holly. "The book on Arthur's lap was put there by the killer."

"Was it?" Julia said, stepping just inside the door.

27

"How can you tell?" Holly said.

"First, it's open to the exact middle, just where someone setting a scene would open it without thinking. Second, even if Arthur *had* been reading that book, how did it magically remain on his lap through the attack? And third, why would Arthur leave Julia to go read a book in the library?"

"He wouldn't," Julia said, nodding in agreement. "When he left, he said he had to do something important. He emphasized that it was important."

I angled my head to read the book's title at the top of open page. "*The Best Slow Cooker Recipes,*" I said aloud.

"There's no way he was reading that," Holly said. "The killer grabbed the nearest book."

I glanced at the shelves directly behind the chair. "There," I said, pointing to a book-sized slot on one shelf.

"We need Chief Gilroy out here right now," Julia said.

An instant later the lights went out.

"You have *got* to be kidding me," Holly said.

CHAPTER 4

Someone down the hall shouted, and I thought I heard Ian yell back, but from where, I couldn't tell. In the dark, sound seemed to have no point of origin. "It must be the storm," I said. "Maybe a tree came down on a power line."

"Unless someone cut the lights," Holly said. "Do you have a flashlight app on your phone?"

"If I had, I would have used it on the stairs. Julia, are you there?"

"I'm in the doorway, and I'm not moving a single inch," she said.

I fumbled my way to the far wall of the library and flung aside the drapes. Though snow clouds obscured the moon, some light reflected off the snow, enabling me to make my way back to Holly without cracking my shins on the furniture. "I'm calling Gilroy," I said, taking my phone from my jeans pocket. The single reception bar didn't bode well, but I tried the call anyway.

"I can't get through," I said after a minute. "I wonder if the land lines are down."

Holly tried her cell phone but didn't fare any better.

"There's a murderer in this house, and the lights have gone off," Julia said in a strangely calm voice.

"We know that, Julia," Holly said.

"I'm just stating the facts."

"We don't need you to do that. We're well aware."

"You know what?" I said. "We're fine. Connie and Ian called the police before the lights went out."

"If they were able to," Julia said. "Do you hear that?"

"Not again," Holly moaned.

"It's not banging, it's . . . footsteps. Where are they coming from?"

I made my way to the door, taking Holly with me. "It's impossible to tell where sounds are coming from in this house."

"Ladies?"

"Shane?" I called.

"That's me. I'm feeling the wall, heading for you. We're off the air until we get the power back."

"Doesn't the hotel have a generator?" Holly said.

"We'll soon find out," I said, squinting down the hall. As my eyes adjusted to the dark, I saw a black form groping the walls, moving our way.

"The hall's darker than room 108," Shane said. "Be careful when you walk back to your rooms, ladies. I tripped over a rug and almost fell on my face."

"Where are the flashlights?" I said.

"The crew is guarding them jealously," Shane replied. "Couldn't pry them out of their hands." When he reached the library door, I saw his face in the meager light from the windows. I didn't know if he was putting on an act for our benefit, but he appeared unflappable, almost as though he'd seen dead men in black-as-night libraries before.

"I thought you should know I contacted the station about Arthur," he said. "You know, to get guidance. So one way or the other, the police know what happened. It'll take time for them to get here in the storm, but they'll be here."

"Oh, that's a relief," Julia said.

"Did the station want you to keep broadcasting?" I asked.

"Oh yeah, the manager did. I told the audience there'd been an incident, but I didn't say what. Keep 'em guessing. That's more provocative than telling them what happened. Plus, that way I don't have to announce Arthur's death over the air. That's a no-good way for relatives to find out. Though I don't even know if he has relatives in the area. Do you?"

I looked at Holly.

"I don't," Holly said. "We talked business when we got together, which wasn't very often. I was thinking a minute ago that I didn't know Arthur very well at all, and he was so supportive of me."

"He liked supporting you," I said.

"He enjoyed your eclairs, I know that," Shane said.

"I would like to get one of your flashlights, if you don't mind," Julia said. "There's no point in everyone in that room having one."

"A woman who speaks her mind," Shane said. "Follow me."

I shut the library door, and the four of us made our way down the hall. I linked arms with Julia, and together we took small, elderly steps, trying not to trip over a rug or each other's feet. As we neared room 108, the hall became brighter and Julia's grip on my arm became less talon-like.

"Here we go, ladies," Shane said. "One of you guys hand me a flashlight if you can spare it."

Conyer reluctantly gave his flashlight to Shane. I guessed that he and Maria were both low on the totem pole compared to Dustin, but Maria was clinging to her flashlight for dear life. She wasn't about to give it up.

"Ma'am," Shane said, transferring the flashlight to Julia.

"Thank you," Julia said. "And thank you, Conyer."

Conyer shrugged.

"What's your name, dear?"

Conyer looked confused. "Conyer."

"I mean your last name. It's nice to know."

"In case we all die?" Maria said.

"Wetzel," Conyer said. "Rhymes with pretzel."

"Yes, I can hear the rhyme for myself, thank you."

"I suggest we conserve battery power," Shane said. "Just one of the flashlights on, all right? Maria? Point yours at the ceiling."

Everyone but Maria dutifully turned their flashlights off, and Maria pointed hers upward. "It works," she said, amazed at the amount of light bouncing off the ceiling.

"Reflection and a white ceiling," Shane said.

It felt as though it had been ages since I'd seen the Swansons, and I was beginning to worry. Not just about them, but about the rest of us. Someone in this hotel was a murderer, and as Julia kept pointing out, we were literally in the dark. "Where are the Swansons?" I said.

"That's a good question," Maria answered. "Aren't they supposed to be taking care of us? Like giving us more flashlights and hot drinks?"

"Or turning on a generator," Holly said. "Where *are* they? They should be caring for their guests."

"I really don't like this," Maria said, as though any of us did.

Shane plopped down on the room's bed. "If we stick

together, we'll be fine."

"Someone here killed that man," Maria countered, tugging at her bright blue headband. She pulled it forward, pushed it back, and tugged again. Playing with it must have comforted her.

"It wasn't one of us," Dustin said. "I didn't even want to come here tonight."

"Neither did I," Maria said.

Conyer simply said, "It's January," and left it at that, as if that were sufficient reason to dislike doing a remote from the Grandview. I supposed it was.

"You know what?" Dustin said, turning his attention to the pastry trays. "These pastries are amazing. You're missing out, Miss Vitamin."

"Knock off calling me that," Maria said. "Just because I like to take care of my health—unlike you."

"I thought you were enjoying the field trip, Maria," Shane said.

"Really, Shane?" Maria said. She joined him on the bed, still clutching the flashlight. "Walking around in a dank basement, chasing air-duct noises? Waiting for a ghost to rise from the grave?"

Shane laughed softly. At least the man had the good graces to see the absurdity in his annual Herbert Purdy show.

"You don't believe in the Purdy ghost, Maria?" Dustin said. "I could swear you did. I saw your face when you heard the bangs."

"Those banging sounds had nothing to do with air ducts," Shane said. "So let's dispense with that right now."

"You're saying it *was* a ghost?" Maria said.

"I'm saying it wasn't ducts," Shane said. "Nothing more complicated than that."

"I agree," I said.

Julia shot me a look.

"I know what a contracting air duct sounds like," I said. "I hear it when I turn the heat down before bed in the winter. The sound we heard was sharper. Like metal hitting concrete."

Shane snapped his fingers. "That's it! I've been trying to find a way to describe it."

"I don't care what the sound was," Holly said with a sigh. "A kind man was just murdered."

"Don't misunderstand," Shane said. "I meant no disrespect to Arthur. I can't speak for everyone, but I'm trying not to think about it. He's down the hall, we're in the dark, and someone in the hotel killed him. I'd rather talk about the show and strange sounds, that's all. I haven't forgotten about him."

"Sure," Holly said. "Whatever you want. Whatever everyone wants."

"The police will be here soon," I said. Though what *soon* meant, I couldn't say. I'd seen a glimpse of the snowstorm from the library window and I knew the roads had to be in rough shape.

"I wonder about that bed," Dustin said, gesturing. "Do you think it's the one Purdy died in?"

Maria scrambled to her feet. "You!"

"That's not helping, Dustin," Shane said. "Maria, take a look. This bed isn't fifty years old. Sit yourself down and relax."

Dustin suddenly turned his face to the door. "I hear a woman calling."

I leaned on the doorjamb, gazed down the hall, and saw a flashlight beam drawing near. Julia flicked on her light and aimed it. "It's Connie and Ian," I said.

"About time," Conyer grumbled. "What a lousy hotel this is."

"Save it for the online review," Maria said. "That's what I plan to do. First thing when I get home."

"There's nothing wrong with the hotel," Holly said. "And it belonged to Arthur, not the Swansons, so think twice before you post a snotty review. He didn't charge you for his rooms, did he? No, I bet he didn't."

Ian reached the door first and began to hand out flashlights on his way to the desk. Once there, he set down a high-beam lantern and turned it on, illuminating the room.

"Sorry, sorry," Connie said. "We've been trying to get the generator going."

"No luck, I take it," Shane said.

"It's being extremely fussy," she said. "We'll try it again later."

It occurred to me with a jolt that Connie might not be telling the truth. Had she and Ian even tried the generator? We didn't even know if there *was* a generator. "Did you call the police?" I asked.

"We never got a chance," Ian said. "The lines are down."

"I thought that's what you went off to do," I said, my possibly irrational irritation with the couple growing. "That was the most important thing. More important than flashlights."

"But the lines were down," Ian said. "I mean, they went down before the lights went out. We checked."

"Oh."

"After the lights went out," Connie said, "we thought we'd work on the generator."

"Oh, I see. Sorry." I was getting testy, like Maria, Julia, and even Holly. I needed James Gilroy. Right now. I'd never thought of myself as being afraid of the dark, but murder put dark in a whole new perspective. It was bad enough being trapped in an isolated hotel with a killer, but a killer you couldn't see? I wanted to hit a switch and flood every room in the place with light.

"Connie, you were telling me earlier about the Purdy murder photos," Shane said.

"Oh, for crying out loud," Maria said. "I can't believe you're asking that now."

"I want her to talk," Shane said. "She told me things I'd never heard before, and I thought I was on top of things."

"Yes, the crime-scene photos we found in the basement last week," Connie said, nodding eagerly. "A remarkable discovery after fifty years."

My ears perked up.

"You were going to show them to me," Shane said.

Connie's face fell. "I'm afraid they're in the library. Ian put them in a photo album so guests could look. I guess I can get them for you."

"No, I will," Ian said, moving for the door.

"We can't take anything from the library," I said. "Wait for the police."

"Rachel's right," Holly said. "It's a crime scene. No one goes in there."

"I hear something," Dustin said, holding a cupped hand to his ear.

The man's hearing was unbelievable. I stuck my head out the door, turned on the flashlight Ian had given me, and directed it down the hall. "I see lights coming from the lobby, nearing the hall."

36

"Where is everyone?" a man groused. "You'd think someone would have met us at the door."

Officer Underhill. Impatient, testy Officer Underhill. I grinned. "It's the police," I said. I hurried for the lobby, reminding myself as I went that Gilroy would object to me hugging and kissing him in front of his officer.

CHAPTER 5

"Are you all right?" Gilroy whispered as Underhill herded us down the hall and into the lobby.

"I'm okay. Everyone is, except for Arthur Jago."

Gilroy nodded, touched the small of my back, and then walked ahead of me. Or hobbled, rather. He was still wearing the fracture boot from December, when he'd broken his ankle after been forced down a canyon road in his cruiser by a lunatic murderer. Thankfully, he'd broken only one bone and could now get about—and rather nicely—without crutches.

Ian had brought the high-beam lantern with him, and when he set it on the coffee table between a pair of old couches, it did a fair job of lighting the lobby. When Dustin and Conyer put their upturned flashlights on the fireplace mantel, only the far corners of the room, off toward the receptionist's desk, were black.

"I'll start a fire," Ian said. "It may be our only heat for a while."

"At least the cold is good for the crime scene," Dustin said. "It keeps the body chilled."

"Arthur isn't a body," Holly snapped. "He was a human being, and someone in this lobby murdered him."

"She's right," Maria said. "There's no way around that.

We can talk about Purdy and ghosts all you want, but someone here is a killer."

I found a seat on one of the lobby's soft but threadbare couches.

"What did you do to your foot, Chief Gilroy?" Shane asked. "Skiing accident?"

"Something like that," Gilroy said.

"So how were the roads?" Shane said. "Are the crime-scene folks going to make it?"

"The county is pulling a plow from the highway to help out," Gilroy said. "But that might not happen until early morning."

"We only made it because we have chains," Underhill said. "It's a nasty storm system."

"You mean we have to stay here?" Conyer asked.

"Where did you think we were going?" Maria said. "Even with the outdoor lights gone you can see the snowstorm."

Conyer dropped dejectedly into one of the couches. "I'd take my chances in a heartbeat. Better the snow than this."

"We're all staying here tonight," Gilroy said. "Underhill, you can start taking statements."

"Oh, man, it's going to be a long night," Conyer said. He took off his glasses and rubbed them on the T-shirt under his sweater.

"The coffee is still warm in the insulated carafes on that table by the windows," Ian said. "Anyone interested?"

"That's a good idea," Gilroy said. "Why don't you pass out the coffee? I'll be back."

Gilroy headed for the library, switching on his department-issue flashlight before he exited the lobby. I wondered what he would make of the crime scene. I closed my eyes, recalling the details I'd committed to memory. More than the book on Arthur's lap was peculiar. Why had the killer stabbed Arthur in the back? And how? *Please lean forward so I can stick a knife in your back. Thank you. Now lean back again.* No, if Arthur had been sitting when he was attacked, a knife in the back made no sense. But if he had been standing . . .

"Coffee, Rachel?" Julia said, nudging my arm. I hadn't even noticed her join me on the couch.

"Yes, please."

Ian handed me a mug, which I gratefully wrapped my cold hands around.

"Holly, can we bring out the rest of your pastries?" Connie asked. "We never did get the chance."

"Pastries?" Underhill said, his pen poised above his notepad.

"Sure, whatever," Holly replied, taking a flashlight with her to the kitchen. "I'll bring them out. Why not eat to our hearts' content?"

"In the meantime, I need everyone's names and addresses," Underhill said. "And I need to know where everyone was before Mr. Jago's body was discovered."

I took a sip of coffee, put down my mug, and went after Holly. We met up in the kitchen as she was piling all the remaining pastries onto one tray. A delicious but precarious pyramid.

"All right, Holly," I said. "What is it?"

"What?" She set a croissant atop the pile. I didn't know how she was going to get the tray into the lobby without dumping half the pastries on the floor.

"It's more than Arthur's death that's making you

angry. You hardly knew him personally."

"All that talk about the *body*," she said. "Like Arthur is a thing. They're thoughtless."

"They don't mean to be. Everyone's scared and speaking without thinking."

Holly's hands dropped to her sides. "What kind of person am I, Rachel?"

I stared.

"I'm asking you a serious question."

"What brought this on?"

"Do you know what my first thought was when I saw Arthur in the library?"

I shook my head.

"I thought, how horrible. That poor man. I wondered if he'd suffered any or if it had happened quickly, before he knew it. Do you know what my second thought was?"

"Tell me."

"The man who wanted to help me expand Holly's Sweets was gone."

"Holly . . ."

"He asked me and Peter to lunch last month, and I said we couldn't, we were too busy."

"December is your busiest month."

"I realize now that I didn't know him. I know he was divorced, but what about kids? Did he have any? I don't know." She wiped her hands on a kitchen towel and then tossed the towel on the counter next to the refrigerator. "The bakery. It's always the bakery with me."

"Holly, stop it. It's your livelihood. More than that, it's your passion. You're *meant* to be a pastry chef, and it's a hard, time-consuming job. Of course you thought of your missed opportunity. It's the reason you came to the

41

Grandview, and it's why Arthur invited you. How could you not think of it?"

"Maybe."

"Did you plan his murder?"

"Don't be silly."

"Would you give up Arthur's help if you could have him back?"

"Yes."

"Then?"

"I feel horrible."

"Which proves you're a good person."

"Am I?"

"You asked me what kind of person you are, and I'm telling you," I said. "And Julia would say the same thing. No, Julia would say something like *Don't you ever ask me such a foolish question again.*"

She smiled. "Okay."

"I mean it."

"Thanks, Rachel."

I grabbed a handful of paper napkins from the counter. "Now let's go before Underhill has a snack attack."

"Did you see his eyes light up when he heard the word 'pastries'?" Holly said. She seized the tray and strode for the lobby, somehow without losing a single pastry from the sugary Matterhorn she'd created.

"Mrs. Kavanagh, those are fantastic looking," Underhill said, following the tray to the coffee table.

"Dig in, Officer," Holly answered. "There are plenty. Don't be shy."

"Is Chief Gilroy still in the library?" I asked Underhill.

"You need to talk to him?"

"For one minute."

42

"Go ahead," he said with a nod.

"A private talk with the chief of police?" Dustin said. "I guess *you're* not a suspect."

Ignoring Dustin, I plucked a donut from the stack of pastries, grabbed a napkin, and set out for the library. I'd forgotten a flashlight, but light from the open library door guided me. When I got there, Gilroy was crouched in front of Arthur Jago, who was now sitting straight in his chair, no longer slumped forward. Gilroy's flashlight was on the floor next to him, pointed at the ceiling.

"I'm guessing you had a good look in here," he said, his eyes trained on Arthur's chest. "Was he bent forward or sitting like this when you found him?"

"Sitting. Just like that. With the book across his lap. When Shane touched him, he fell forward. No one touched him after that."

Gilroy stood, grunting slightly with the effort, and continued to stare at Arthur's body.

"Do you think it's strange he was stabbed in the back?" I asked.

"Yup."

"And with a book about slow cooker recipes on his lap."

"Yeah."

"He fell into the chair or he was put there after he was stabbed."

"Probably."

Short answers. Gilroy's detective brain was in high gear. I needed to leave him to his business. I desperately wanted a look at the Purdy photo album Ian had put together, but I figured it was best to wait until the coroner took Arthur's body away. From where I was standing, I couldn't see where the album was, and I sure wasn't going to scour the shelves while the crime scene was still active. "I'll leave your donut on a napkin outside the door," I said.

"Thanks, Rachel. Would you ask Underhill to bring his camera and get the ultraviolet flashlight?"

"Um . . . sure."

Gilroy's eyes were still fixed on Arthur's chest when I left. Whatever he was seeing, or hoping to see, was a mystery to me.

Back in the lobby, I told Underhill about the camera and flashlight. Judging by the officer's grimace, the request involved a trip to the squad car in the snowstorm. "I'll save you a bear claw," I said.

Underhill grunted and zipped up his coat.

While I saved a bear claw for Underhill, I snatched the lone cream puff on the tray for myself. Holly she'd stashed more in her suitcase, but it was going to be a while before we could retire to our rooms—our *dark* rooms—and I needed my pastry. "Has anyone heard more strange noises?" I said before taking a bite.

"Come to think of it, no," Shane said, thoughtfully rubbing his chin.

"Where's the ghost of Herbert Purdy?" Conyer said. He was working on another cinnamon-honey roll, I noticed. Pastry-wise, he was putting me to shame.

"We have a murderer in our midst," Julia said. "We don't need a ghost on top of that."

"Maybe the ghost is the murderer," Conyer said. "He stabs people in the back just like he was stabbed in the back. It's his weird revenge. Guests beware."

Connie groaned in disgust. "This is the Grandview, not Murder Hotel."

"Isn't your whole marketing plan based on selling the Grandview as Murder Hotel?" Dustin said. "And that *was* the hotel's knife in Arthur's back. You said it was."

"Anyone could have taken that," Connie said. She sighed sadly and looked about the lobby. "This could be such a bright and beautiful place."

"Don't wish for something you can't have," Dustin said. "What you've got here is Murder Hotel. Make do with what you've got. That's what Arthur was doing, it seems to me. Making the best of the hotel's reputation, and making a lot of money in the process."

Connie looked ready to hand Dustin a tongue-lashing, but whatever she was about to say was interrupted by Underhill's noisy return.

"It's really coming down," he said, shaking the snow from his coat and stomping his feet on the entrance mat. "I kind of hoped the coroner would make it, but not tonight he won't."

"That figures," Conyer said.

Mumbling, "It's going to be a long night," Underhill headed for the library, camera and flashlight in hand.

Julia leaned sideways and whispered. "What is the ultraviolet flashlight for?"

"That's what I want to know." I was dying to find out. I snagged Underhill a bear claw, plopped it on a napkin, and set off for the library. This was borderline behavior—intruding on Gilroy's territory. He no longer called my sideline investigations "meddling," and he had even asked my opinion on cases, but this was a crime scene and I was clearly snooping—with pastry in hand.

Gilroy had switched off his regular flashlight and was bent toward Arthur, training the ultraviolet light on his chest, when I got to the library. The front of Arthur's sweater was faintly smudged with something that glowed a soft whitish yellow under the light—and had been all but invisible under regular light. Especially on the sweater's outrageously bold print. The book on his lap also bore a few small, glowing smudges on its open pages.

"What is it?" Underhill asked as he snapped a photo of the book.

"Food, maybe. Was he eating?" Gilroy said, glancing over at me.

"Arthur was pretty heavy into the eclairs," I said. "But I don't see any crumbs."

"It's not crumbs," Gilroy said. He straightened and shot a look at the bear claw in my hand. "Hold that up, Rachel."

When I held out my hand, Gilroy directed his light at the bear claw. The entire top of it glowed with the same whitish yellow.

"Radioactive pastry, who would've thought?" Underhill said.

Gilroy flicked on his other flashlight before turning off the ultraviolet. "Underhill, take what photos you can in this light and then keep an eye on the lobby."

"Yes, Chief."

"And Rachel," Gilroy added, handing me his flashlight, "would you ask Mrs. Kavanagh to come back here? She doesn't have to come in the library. I'll meet her in the hall."

CHAPTER 6

"That's the glaze on the bear claw," Holly said, shooting miserable glances at the library door. "Honey and maple syrup glow under ultraviolet light."

Though Gilroy had waited for Holly in the dark hall, away from the library, she was still uneasy. So was I, truth be told. I wanted the lights to come back on, and I wanted the coroner to come and move poor Arthur's body. Gilroy's regular flashlight had lit the way ahead as Holly and I left the lobby, but the blackness had pressed in behind us. I knew Holly had felt it too. We had quickened our steps, and I'd called out for James. How he could wait for us in the darkness bewildered me. The man seemed to know no fear.

"I've read that tonic water and some soaps and detergents glow, but I didn't know honey and maple syrup did," Gilroy said.

"They don't glow very brightly," Holly said. "Not like tonic water."

"What about eclairs?" Gilroy asked. "Any ingredients that glow?"

"No, nothing. The only pastries I brought that would react that way are the bear claws and cinnamon-honey rolls."

"Do you know if Mr. Jago ate either of those?"

Holly glanced at me. I shook my head.

47

"I don't think he did, Chief," Holly said. "Eclairs were his favorite. If the night had gone on, he might have tried other pastries, but he was waiting for the eclairs. He asked me specifically for them, and I saw him eating one in room 108."

"Okay, thank you."

"Someone touched him on his chest or pushed him," I said. "Maybe threatened him at some point."

Underhill looked up from his work.

"Let's keep this to ourselves," Gilroy said.

"We're stuck here all night for sure, aren't we?" Holly said.

"It looks that way. I think you, Rachel, and Mrs. Foster should stay in one room—or in the lobby. Either way. But not in separate rooms. Don't separate at all, in fact. Stick together at all times."

"You don't have to convince us," I said. "What about you and Underhill?"

"We'll stay in the lobby. Awake."

Back on the couch in the lobby, I drank what was left of my now-cool coffee and told Julia that Gilroy said we should stick together tonight. No separate rooms, no walking around by ourselves. She readily agreed. "But let's stay in my room," she said. "It's farthest from *that* room."

Holly nudged Julia closer to me and took a seat at the other end of the couch.

"We've got more serious problems than room 108," I said under my breath.

"Like we might freeze to death before the night is over," Julia said, rubbing her arms to keep warm.

"Cold?" Shane asked, rising from his chair. "There's a blanket on the couch table behind you."

"Oh, you don't need to—"

"My pleasure," he said, handing Julia a fleecy throw. "So what do you think, ladies?" He sank back into his chair.

"About?" I said.

"Let's start with Herbert Purdy."

"Heavens, we'll never be free," Julia said.

Shane smiled at Julia and shook a finger at me. "I've read about you in the *Juniper Grove Post*, Rachel Stowe. You're no ordinary observer."

"You're right about that," Underhill said. Back from taking photos in the library, he took a huge bite of his bear claw and reached for his coffee to wash it down.

"Don't believe what you read in the papers," I said.

"I'd value your opinion, Rachel. I'd like to give my listeners a new perspective on the case, not the same thing year after year, and assuming we get back to Fort Collins in time, I'll be talking about Purdy on my show tomorrow night. I'll need to make up for tonight's disaster."

"All I know about the Purdy murder is what Connie told us when we arrived."

Hearing her name, Connie swiveled in her chair by the fireplace. "More Purdy?" she said, looking back at our little group.

"Come on over here," Shane said. "What can you tell us that we don't know?"

Connie left Ian, and her toasty chair by the fire, and took a seat near Shane. "I'm not an expert, and unfortunately, fifty years ago, crime-scene analysis wasn't as advanced as it is now. The police fingerprinted all the guests and employees, and only the employees' prints were found in Purdy's room. But that's to be expected."

For someone who professed to hate the Grandview's

49

reputation as Murder Hotel, Connie had enthusiastically joined the conversation.

"What about fingerprints on the knife?" I asked.

"There were no prints on the knife," Shane said. "But what killer with half a brain would leave his prints on the murder weapon?"

"Gloves," Connie said with a definitive nod. "The killer wore gloves the entire time he was in Purdy's room."

"So Purdy is in his pajamas, either about to go to bed or already in bed," I said. "Someone knocks on the door. Purdy opens it, and he not only allows this glove-wearing killer into his room but he turns his back on him?"

I caught a flicker of a smile on Shane's face.

"It could have been a maid or other staff member," Connie said.

"Wearing gloves and knocking on his door at bedtime?" I said. "At any hotel I've ever stayed at, the maids are finished with the rooms by afternoon. After that, they don't disturb the guests."

"Maybe he asked for fresh towels," Connie suggested.

"And the maid brought them wearing gloves? Weren't there already towels in the room?"

"The only towels in the crime-scene photos were in the bathroom," Connie said.

"I want to see those new photographs," Shane said. "I've got a feeling about them."

"Did the police question the maids?" I asked.

"They questioned everyone at the hotel, employees and guests," Shane said. "Twenty-two people in all. No one knew Purdy or had the smallest connection to him. Or that's what they claimed."

"They didn't have Internet searches back then," Maria

chimed in as she perused what was left of the pastries. "If they said they had no connection, the police had to believe them or travel who knows how far and interview other people."

"I thought you didn't eat sugar," Dustin said.

"I make an exception when I'm starving."

"The guests could have lied about knowing Purdy," Shane said, "and the police would've been none the wiser."

"Just because it was fifty years ago doesn't mean they were all fools," I said. "They must have checked people's backgrounds."

Connie leaned forward, a kind of frantic delight in her expression. "Did you know the police searched room 108 for secret passages? The room was carpeted at the time, and they tore the entire carpet up, thinking there was a secret way from the room to the basement. That was one of their theories on how the killer escaped without being noticed by anyone else on the first floor."

"And there was no escape hatch?" Shane said. "What a shock."

"It was a solid wood floor."

Maria tore the curved end from a chocolate croissant and stuffed it in her mouth. It was the first I'd seen her eat since arriving at the Grandview. Conyer was watching her too. His appetite spurred, he rose from his seat on a couch near the fireplace and wandered over to the coffee table. His lips pursed in concentration, he stared down at the pastry tray.

"Go ahead," Shane said. "I'm not having any more. Ladies?"

"No thanks," Holly said. I could tell her mood had lightened, but it was way past her baker's bedtime, and she was fighting to stay awake. I gave her half an hour before she fell asleep sitting up.

Conyer reached for the remaining bear claw. "Has anyone considered the similarities between Arthur's death and Purdy's death?"

"It's strange Arthur was stabbed in the back on the fiftieth anniversary of Purdy's death," Shane said. "I'll give you that."

"But the library door was open when I found Arthur," Connie said. "Unlike room 108's locked door. Anyway, the library door doesn't lock. Anyone could have gone in there."

"Anyone could have gone into Purdy's room," I reminded her. "Anyone at the hotel could have killed him."

"But his door was locked," Shane said. "The manager had to open it the next morning."

I pointed out that a locked door the next morning meant nothing. It didn't mean Purdy's door was locked the night before—not that a locked hotel door would have prevented a staff member or guest from gaining access to Purdy's room. And it didn't mean that Purdy didn't open the door to his killer—who then locked the door on his way out. "There are only three suspicious things about Purdy's death. He was in his pajamas, he was stabbed in the back, and he was found face down in the middle of his bed."

"I've never given the pajamas much thought," Shane said. "People wear pajamas in a hotel."

Proclaiming my need for coffee, I took my mug and a flashlight to the table by the windows and managed to pump a few ounces from one of the carafes. Frigid air seeped in through the old window frames, chilling me. The coffee, even if it was still slightly warm, wasn't going to help much. But I had an ulterior motive for leaving my seat on the couch.

Underhill had stationed himself by the coffee, and I wanted his permission to talk to Gilroy again before he sealed off the library for the night.

I whispered to Underhill, he nodded, and I exited the lobby.

Gilroy was running his ultraviolet flashlight over the library's oriental rug when I knocked on the doorjamb. The near-absolute darkness of the hall, Arthur's body—hidden from my view but a presence nonetheless—and Gilroy's eerie purple light gave me a major case of the creeps. "I was wondering if I could borrow a photo album Connie Swanson said was in here."

"I can't let you do that, Rachel," Gilroy said. "Everything needs to stay in place for the coroner and better photos in the daylight."

"I figured. But I thought I'd try."

"Why is it so important?"

I told Gilroy how the Swansons had discovered the Purdy crime-scene photos in the basement, and about my niggling suspicion that Herbert Purdy's and Arthur Jago's murders were connected in some bizarre way. Purdy and Jago—both stabbed in the back at the Grandview Hotel, exactly fifty years apart. I didn't believe in coincidences.

"Hang on." He scanned the bookshelves and found what looked like a yellow fake-leather photo album on a shelf opposite Arthur's body. Still wearing his latex gloves, he slid it out and examined it with his ultraviolet light. Four tiny smudges glowed near the album's spine. "That's strange," he mumbled. He laid the album open in his hands and held it before me while I stood in the doorway. "I'll turn the pages, you look."

I pulled my phone from my pocket, and not hearing

any objections from Gilroy, I started snapping photos. Though Connie had said the album contained crime-scene photos, the photos' clarity surprised me. Someone had used a quality camera and taken high-resolution color shots of everything in the room, from the door to the windows, the bed, the dresser, and the bathroom.

There was even a closeup of the doorframe and door lock, as if to say, *See? No one jimmied the lock or broke down the door. It really is a locked-room mystery.* And the police had indeed removed the room's carpet, because while the first photo in the album showed a fully carpeted room, a later photo, with Purdy's body gone, showed wooden floors.

"Can you go back to the first photo?"

Gilroy flipped the pages.

There was Purdy, face down on the bed, the murder weapon in his back, but slightly off center. "What kind of knife is that? A kitchen knife?"

"Hard to tell."

"Purdy's bed isn't made. He was ready for bed, but he never got in it."

"Looks like it."

"One stab wound?"

"If the knife was long enough, it punctured his lung and one wound was all it took."

"That could mean the killer had to wait around to make sure Purdy died."

"That would be the smart thing to do."

"Wouldn't it have been smarter to stab him multiple times?"

"Maybe the killer couldn't bring himself to do that. Especially if he knew Purdy." Gilroy put the album back on the shelf and then shut the library door behind him. We stood silently in the hall, his ultraviolet beam our only light. Exhaustion was setting in for both of us.

"I'm glad you're here," I said.

He gathered me in his arms, and for a moment, Arthur Jago, Herbert Purdy, and the drafty halls of the Grandview Hotel disappeared.

"Don't leave your friends tonight, Rachel," he said. "No matter where I go. Don't leave them, and don't let them leave you."

CHAPTER 7

Twenty minutes later, Shane and his crew toddled off to their separate bedrooms, and Julia, Holly, and I grabbed our coats from our own rooms and locked ourselves in Julia's room. Aware of how ineffectual a Grandview lock could be, I wedged a straight-backed chair under the doorknob for extra measure. Julia flung open the room's drapes and set her flashlight atop the room's bureau, aiming the beam at the ceiling.

"I am *so* tired," Holly said, dropping to the bed and wrapping the bedspread around her shoulders. She lay on her side, drew up her feet, and threw the bedspread across her legs.

"Holly, your shoes are still on," Julia said.

"I don't care. I'm not moving until morning."

Tired as I was, I was more interested in mulling over Arthur's and Purdy's murders than in going to sleep, so I told Julia to take the other side of the bed. I slipped into my coat—it was only going to get colder in our room—and then found a pen and Grandview notepad in the bureau, sat in the room's one comfortable armchair, and propped my feet on the end of the bed. Starting with Arthur's murder, I listed the suspects—Shane and his radio crew, and Connie and Ian Swanson.

If either of the Swansons had a motive for killing Arthur, they'd had plenty of opportunity to kill before. But maybe they had waited for the anniversary of Purdy's murder because it muddied the investigatory waters. Or maybe there had been bad blood between Arthur and them and it had finally boiled over with the stress of the remote radio broadcast.

"I hear doors opening," Julia said.

"Maybe people are getting food in the kitchen," I said.

One thing I knew: Connie was ambivalent at best about the Grandview's reputation. On the one hand, she liked to say the hotel would make a lovely getaway if only people would forget the Purdy murder, but on the other hand, she and Ian had stocked the library with disconcerting photos of the Purdy crime scene. Strange behavior for the manager of a getaway.

Connie and Ian had probably felt themselves between a rock and a hard place. Unable to persuade Arthur to turn the Grandview into a bright and modern hotel, to divorce it from its grisly past, they had decided to make the most of the Purdy murder. It paid their bills. And now, sadly, Arthur's death would add to the Grandview's reputation.

Shane, too, had a stake in the Grandview remaining Murder Hotel, though even without his annual Purdy broadcast, his radio show was popular. But reading between the lines, the remote show brought huge ad revenues to the station and ensured Shane's continued employment. Arthur Jago was no threat to him or his livelihood. If anything, Arthur was Shane's benefactor. The hotel's next owner might stop the broadcasts altogether—and even wipe out Purdy's memory. *If I owned this place, that's what I'd do*, I thought.

No one on Shane's crew seemed happy to be at the Grandview, but one night in a creepy hotel wasn't reason enough to murder the hotel's owner. Or even murder Shane.

Had the crew been to the Grandview before? Thinking back to the way Maria had reacted to Dustin's taunt about her sitting on the bed Purdy had died in, it was hard to believe she'd been in the room before. All of it seemed new and disturbingly macabre to her. Dustin, on the other hand, was the engineer, and probably not a newbie to Shane's show.

Finally giving in to the late hour, I rested my head on the chair back and shut my eyes. Someone in this hotel was a killer. Were we in for a peaceful night or would he strike again? I drifted off to sleep, secure in the knowledge that Gilroy and Underhill weren't sleeping.

Sometime later, I woke slowly to a distant clanging sound.

"Rachel?" Julia whispered. She was wide awake, sitting straight up in bed.

"I hear it." I swung my feet from the bed.

"Where is it coming from?"

My eyes rose to the ceiling. "Upstairs?" I checked my watch. "It's two in the morning. I've only been asleep an hour."

"It sounded like it was coming from the basement before. Didn't it?"

"It's impossible to tell."

"I'm going to kill whoever is making that noise," Holly mumbled.

"Connie Swanson has a nerve saying that's a contracting air duct," Julia said.

"Even if it was, the heat was turned down hours ago

58

and then the power went out," I said. "The ducts wouldn't still be making noises."

Holly sat up with a groan and pulled the bedspread under her chin. "I don't suppose I'm going to sleep."

I walked to the door and slid the high-backed chair from under the knob.

"Where do you think you're going?" Julia said. "You are *not* leaving this room."

"Keep your voice down. I'm just going to listen."

In a second, Holly was at my side.

"You two," Julia hissed. "If you get us killed."

"No one's going to die," I whispered.

"Those were probably Arthur Jago's last words," Julia said.

I opened the door part way, and Holly and I peered into the darkness.

"It stopped," Holly said under her breath. "No, wait. There it is."

The clanging began again, though to my ears it seemed no louder than before. "I don't think it's coming from this floor."

I tiptoed into the hall, Holly behind me.

"Oh, honestly," Julia huffed. "With a murderer on the loose."

"It doesn't seem to be coming from room 108," Holly said.

I heard Julia's feet hit the floor. "You're not leaving me by myself."

The three of us stood in the doorway, trying to determine where the sound was coming from.

"Could it be the basement again?" Julia said.

"I don't think it was the basement the first time," Holly

said.

"The flashlight," I said, heading back into the room. I needed to know that Gilroy heard the noise, and he needed to know that Arthur had been murdered shortly after the first time we heard that same noise. I started again for the hall, but Julia caught my arm and stopped me.

"You can't go out there," she said.

"Julia, that noise is connected to Arthur's murder, and I need to tell Gilroy."

"But we stay together," Holly said.

"Get your coats, and Julia, put your shoes on." I aimed the flashlight into the room.

"This is madness," Julia said, pulling her shoes from under the bed. "What would Chief Gilroy say? Never mind. I know what he'd say. I can just hear him now."

Holly put on her coat and joined me at the door. "Julia, all we're going to do is walk to the lobby and tell him about that noise," she said. "He may think it's nothing but old-house noises, and he needs to know it could be significant."

Tugging on Julia's coat sleeve, I pulled her into the hall and then shut the door. "Look at it this way. Maybe he and Underhill can find the source of the sound and we can finally get some sleep."

I pointed the flashlight down the long hall, shining it into the blackness, and the three of us stepped tentatively toward the lobby. Julia twitched like a nervous hen, hesitating, moving again, looking over her shoulder. As we drew closer and my eyes adjusted to the dark, I realized the high-beam lantern Ian had placed on the coffee table had been turned off—or taken to someone's room. Not even the faintest light shone from the lobby. It was as perfectly black as the hall.

When we rounded the corner into the lobby, I did a quick scan with the flashlight. The lantern was gone, the fire had shriveled to embers.

"Where are Gilroy and Underhill?" Holly breathed.

"Maybe they're hunting for the noise," I said. "What's that weird smell?"

"Like an old furnace smell?" Holly said.

"Not quite. Besides, the furnace isn't on."

"I don't like this," Julia said. "I keep feeling something behind me. Like it's creeping up on me. Don't you feel that?"

I spun back, swung around the corner, and directed the beam down the hall. Nothing. I was about to turn back to the lobby when the sound of a door creaking froze me in place. An instant later, a dim shaft of light emerged from one of the rooms. "Who is it?" I called out, long past caring if I woke anyone.

A dark figure stepped into the hall, pointed a flashlight my way, and then tilted the beam upward, lighting up his face. "It's Shane. I heard something."

"That banging again," I said.

"You realize he could be the murderer," Julia whispered in my ear.

"I've made it my life's mission not to murder anyone, Miss Julia," Shane said, heading toward us, his flashlight pointed downward, illuminating his steps.

"How did you hear that?" Julia said.

"What can I say? I have good hearing. It's handy in my business." He walked past us into the lobby, shot his flashlight around the room, and then aimed it at the ceiling. "Where are the cops? I thought they were going to stay in the lobby."

"They're in the kitchen," Julia said. "They'll be out any

second now, so you stay right where you are."

Shane raised his eyebrows. "Now, Julia, you really think I'm a murderer?"

"Why wouldn't you be?" I said, coming alongside Julia.

"You too, Rachel?"

"It's you or one of your crew," I said.

"You forget the Swansons."

"So you admit it could be one of your crew."

Shane chuckled. "You should be a lawyer."

"Have Dustin, Maria, and Conyer all been here before?" I asked.

"Only Dustin. Why?"

"How well do you know them?"

The smile vanished from Shane's face. "I don't hire murderers. But have you considered that maybe Arthur did? Not on purpose, naturally."

"Do you suspect Ian and Connie?" Holly asked.

"I don't suspect anyone."

"That's very charitable of you," Holly said, "but someone in this hotel killed Arthur."

Suddenly Shane threw a finger to his lips. "Shh."

Julia clutched at me, her nails like barbs in my shoulder.

"Lights out," I whispered, flicking off my flashlight. Shane followed suit.

I could hear a muffled voice coming from beyond the lobby and the soft thud of footsteps, both growing louder with each second. I leaned close to Holly and mouthed Connie's name. She nodded.

"We have to finish this tonight," Connie was saying.

I caught sight of her between the front door and the

receptionist desk. The four of us huddled close together. Barely breathing, we hoped the dark would shield us.

Ian Swanson came alongside his wife. "Where are the cops? I thought they were camping out in the lobby."

"What do you wanna bet they went to bed?"

"Aren't you tired, Connie? I think this can wait. I'm sick of digging holes."

Holly's eyes grew wide.

"Cops are going to be all over this place by morning," Connie said. "We need to do it now."

"We don't even know if anything's there," Ian said. "We should have waited."

"No, it was perfect timing."

"Perfect timing? With the cops sleeping in the lobby? I say we wait. Better safe than sorry."

"Ian, come on. It's our big chance."

A bang sounded from somewhere in the hotel—the same metal-on-concrete sound as before, only louder this time.

"No," Connie said, her head jerking as another bang resonated. "How can that be? Who's up there?"

"Up the back stairs," Ian said, seizing his wife's hand and rushing out of the lobby.

I switched on my flashlight. "I knew it. It was them."

"What are you talking about?" Shane said.

"Connie and Ian were making that noise. Now someone else is, and I think I know who."

"Were they trying to scare the guests?" Shane said.

"No, I don't think so. That was just a happy consequence. My guess is they found something else along with the crime-scene photos and they're trying to unearth it."

"But they found the photos in the basement," Shane

said.

"The photos suddenly appear after fifty years?" I said, shaking my head. "They weren't in the basement. If they had been, they would've been found long ago."

"So who's up there now?" Julia asked.

"Gilroy and Underhill."

"You sound very sure of things," Shane said.

I pointed my flashlight's beam behind me. "Where are the stairs?"

"The public stairs are at the far end of that hall," Shane said, "but the Swansons took the old room-service stairs, through the kitchen. Let's go. I want to nail those two. They owe me a night's sleep."

"Wait a second." I had seen it as I walked up the hall with Julia and Holly—the thing that was off, that wasn't right—but until that moment, my brain hadn't registered it. Now, as I pointed the flashlight toward the hall, I realized what it was. The door was open only a sliver, but it shouldn't have been open at all. Gilroy had shut it firmly. "It's the library door," I said. "It's open."

CHAPTER 8

The clanging ceased moments after Ian and Connie ran from the lobby, and since I was sure Gilroy had things under control upstairs, I decided—to Julia's horror—to check out the library door rather than find him and Underhill. Shane, on the other hand, looked ready to give the Swansons a major chewing-out and headed for the room-service stairs in the kitchen.

The library door was open an inch, that's all, but it hadn't opened itself. I'd closed that door myself, before Gilroy arrived, and it had closed solidly, firmly. Someone had opened the door after we'd all gone to bed.

"Do you think Arthur is still in there?" Julia said, hovering behind me.

"Where else would he be?" Holly said.

"For all I know someone moved him," Julia said. "I wouldn't put it past this bunch. Or maybe he got up and moved himself. That wouldn't surprise me either."

"Julia, really," Holly said.

"I can't help it. It's this place. It does things to my imagination."

"It's all right," I said. "We all feel the same."

"But I'm imagining things. That's only the first step, you know. Next I'll be *seeing* things."

"You heard doors opening, and that wasn't imagining things. I told you it was probably people going to the kitchen." I shook my head and pushed open the door. "I was wrong. Stay outside the library and keep watch."

"You shouldn't go in," Holly said.

"Gilroy would kill me, I know. Give me one minute."

Julia's fear that Arthur's body had magically left the library had spooked me a little, so the first thing I did was train the flashlight on the armchair.

"Is Arthur . . . ?" Holly said.

"He's still here." I felt ridiculous saying that. Of course he was still there. His fleshy face seemed to have sagged a little, making him look less frightened in death, but maybe that was a trick of the light and shadows. At the very least the man had died in shock. But then a lethal stab wound was a shocking thing.

I ran my light over the library furniture and shelves, looking for anything missing, anything disturbed. At first I couldn't imagine anyone except the killer reentering the library, but I remembered that Shane and his crew were news people at heart. News people meant scoop people, and Arthur's death was a scoop that was hard to resist.

Next I cast my light on the floor, but the oriental rug looked the same as earlier. No one had dropped a cigarette on it or stained it with muddy footprints. Nothing so easy or obvious.

I trained my light on Arthur again. Had someone ventured into the library to take a photo of him? It was almost unthinkable. But Shane was a hard-working man, an ambitious man, and he might have looked to the future and seen twice the ratings in an anniversary show next year. Two January murders, fifty years apart. Had Shane or his crew taken a photo of poor, dead Arthur? Or of the murder room for a future broadcast?

Then it hit me. *Photos*. I aimed the beam at the bookcase opposite Arthur's chair.

The yellow photo album was gone.

I exited the library and pulled the door toward me, leaving it open an inch, just as before.

"I hear Gilroy," Holly said. "His ankle boot thumps when he walks."

"Oh, thank goodness," Julia said. "Some sanity."

Gilroy's voice sounded from the other end of the hall, and seconds later he and Underhill came into sight, Underhill bearing the bright lantern before them. As they trod down the hall, Shane and the Swansons behind them, more doors opened and heads popped out of them.

"What is all the noise?" Maria complained.

"You're just now hearing it?" Shane said. "We've been up for ages, and you've missed a lot."

"When I get home, I'm buying one of those high-beam things," Holly said as Underhill approached. "This hotel doesn't even have battery-lit exit signs. It has to be illegal. Imagine if there was a fire."

That was it. That was the weird smell. "There might be something left of it," I said, racing off and leaving Julia and Holly staring after me.

I cut across the lobby for the fireplace, hoping to find something left of the photo album, but when I got there, all that visibly remained of its pages and photos were strings and puddles of melted plastic. Irretrievable. The yellow album itself wasn't in or around the fire, or anywhere I directed my light.

"What is it, Rachel?" Gilroy said.

I looked back. "Someone destroyed the Herbert Purdy crime-scene photos."

Gilroy took hold of Underhill's lantern and joined me at the fireplace, his eyes wandering over the scene as he moved the light back and forth over the fire, hearth, and surrounding floor.

"I don't see the yellow album anywhere," I added.

"How do you know that glob in the fireplace is the photos?"

"Holly, Julia, and I heard the noise just now, and we wanted to tell you we'd heard it earlier—just before Arthur was killed. We came to the lobby to look for you, and I noticed the library door was open."

Gilroy lowered the lantern. "And you had a look in the library."

I grimaced. "I couldn't help it."

"So someone took advantage of the noise distraction on the third floor to get into the library," he said.

"They probably thought it was safer not to shut the door all the way. Everything echoes in this place. Did you find Connie and Ian upstairs?"

Gilroy's eyes narrowed and a faint smile played on his lips. "You guessed right. They won't tell me what they were looking for."

"Did you lure them upstairs by banging on something?"

"They were breaking up an old brick fireplace. I hit it a few times with their sledgehammer to see how they'd react to the noise."

It was my turn to smile. I shot a glance over my shoulder. The Swansons, looking properly chastised, were seated together on a couch. Connie smoothed her skirt, working out her anxiety on the fabric, and Ian ran his fingers through his short brown hair.

Across the coffee table from the Swansons, Underhill was on another couch, drinking what must have been a very cold cup of coffee. On the other side of the lobby, Dustin, Maria, and Conyer were talking quietly with Shane, who no doubt was filling them in on what they had missed.

"I wonder if those photos could have told us what the Swansons were looking for," I said, keeping my voice low. "Connie said they found them last week."

"I wonder."

"Luckily, I have copies on my phone."

"Yes, I believe you do."

"Though *where* the Swansons found the photos might be the answer to our questions. Where was this fireplace they were breaking up?"

"In room 311."

The number rang a bell. "Al Capone's men kept a lookout in that room way back when. Capone himself stayed in 312."

"More and more interesting. I think I'll go have a talk with them."

Gilroy walked up to the Swanson's couch, set his lantern down on the coffee table, and sat next to it, staring silently at the couple.

Unnerved, Ian became twitchy, looking anywhere but at Gilroy. "Yes?" he said after a moment.

"No more games, no more lies," Gilroy said. "This is a murder investigation."

"We didn't kill Arthur," Ian protested. "I'll tell you that right now."

"You've been lying to me. It's called obstruction of

69

justice."

"This has nothing to do with Arthur," Connie said, her voice wavering. "Honestly, it doesn't. He was our friend."

"You don't get to decide what you tell the truth about. What were you doing in room 311?"

From the corner of my eye, I saw Shane, riveted to the conversation, edge closer to Gilroy, making sure he caught every word.

"We can't do a little after-hours renovation?" Connie said, her mouth twisting in a crooked smile.

I winced. Gilroy wasn't in the mood for slick humor.

"That's enough, Mrs. Swanson," he said.

Ian leapt in. "All right, fine. We found the Purdy photos stuffed up the old fireplace. We thought it was weird. Right, Connie?" He looked to his wife.

"Yes, to find them after all these years," she said. "No one's seen them since the investigation. It was a coup for the hotel. Arthur went crazy over them and told Ian to put them on display in an album."

"The only reason we found them is because we were trying to see if the fireplace could be restored, but with a new surround," Ian said.

Connie nodded. "We were taking it apart anyway, and Arthur was fine with that. He gave us permission, so we weren't breaking any law by tearing it down."

"It turns out it's not a working fireplace, but someone hid the photos between the brick surround and the fake vent—you know, the hole that's supposed to go up a chimney. Know what I mean?"

"Yes, I know the hole that's supposed to go up a chimney," Gilroy said.

Ian bit the inside of his lower lip.

70

"And you thought with the hotel emptied of guests," Gilroy went on, "except for ones expecting some ghostly noises in the night, you'd get on with your renovation."

"Yes," Ian said meekly. "We thought everybody would head down to the basement if we hinted that the banging was coming from the air ducts. That would leave us free to get on with things before the Purdy anniversary ended."

"We thought it was good timing," Connie said. "All the other hotel guests were gone, and the radio audience expected strange sounds. We were helping out, if you think about it. We were adding atmosphere. Everybody enjoyed themselves."

"What did you think you'd find in the fireplace?" Shane said.

Gilroy turned and gave him a sharp look. "Mr. Rooney."

"Sorry, sorry." Shane held up his hands, palms out, and backed off.

"We didn't kill Arthur," Ian said. "He gave us this job, he paid us well, we live in the suite on the third floor"—he pointed feebly at the ceiling—"and it's nicer than any apartment we could afford. We liked him. We have a life here."

"Did you tell Mr. Jago you found the photos in room 311?" Gilroy said.

Connie hung her head. "We said we found them in the basement. We told everybody that."

"So you could keep anything else you found in the room to yourselves," Gilroy said.

After a moment's hesitation, Connie relented. "Yeah."

"And have you found anything else?" Gilroy said.

"We haven't," Ian said adamantly. "Nothing. Just old

71

bricks and mortar."

"And you're going to give me permission to search your suite," Gilroy said. He wasn't asking a question—or asking their permission. He was flat-out telling them what he intended to do, and they were expected to comply.

"Of course," Ian said.

"But Ian . . . ," Connie began.

"We have nothing to hide," Ian said. "And I have a feeling we'll be in a better position if we cooperate. Am I right, Chief Gilroy?"

Gilroy stood. "I think I can look past the obstruction charge. What the hotel's new owner wants to do with you after that isn't my business."

Ian dug into his jeans pocket and handed Gilroy a key. "The door is labeled Suite 3."

"Take a seat, everyone," Gilroy said, looking around the room. "This time, no one leaves the lobby."

CHAPTER 9

The pale winter sun was slanting through the hotel lobby's windows when I woke. Hours of sitting on the couch, crunched between Julia and Holly, had left me sore, but I was wrapped in both my coat and the bedspread from my room and so toasty warm I was reluctant to move. After Gilroy had insisted that everyone spend the night in the lobby, Underhill had made several trips to the bedrooms to bring back coats, blankets, and pillows. I had considered sleeping on the floor—at least there I could stretch out—but I knew I would regret a night on cold wood planks and thin rugs even more than a night sitting stiffly on an old couch.

Gilroy was outside pacing and hobbling, probably waiting for the coroner or the power company. I could only see him above the waist, but he walked like a man slogging through snowdrifts. And a man who hadn't slept all night. Underhill, fast asleep and snoring, his head resting against the wall, was sitting by the door in a wooden chair brought from the kitchen. He was younger than me, and certainly fitter, but he too was going to be sore when he woke.

I stretched a little, testing my bones and muscles before I stood. *I have to start exercising*. It wasn't just the extra twenty-five pounds I carried and still hadn't shed, it was my increasingly sedentary life. When I wasn't sniffing out killers, I was sitting in my home office, pounding out mystery novels, hour after hour. I'd been promising myself for months that I'd start walking the lovely trail behind my house, but so far the gumption to do so had eluded me. Gilroy was five years older than me but trimmer and healthier. I had some work to do.

I made my way to the door—not without discomfort—and went outside. Gilroy smiled when he saw me, but we avoided greeting each other with a kiss or hug. He was on the job, after all.

The sight of Gilroy and the morning light, gray as it was, instantly lifted my spirits—until I remembered poor Arthur Jago in the library. Eight or ten inches of snow had fallen overnight, not enough to knock out power in a town like Juniper Grove, but the foothills were another world. A pine tree, weighted down by the snow, could fall on a line and take out power for miles.

Gilroy followed me as I trudged through foot-plus drifts to the side of the hotel to check on Holly's car. It looked like a giant marshmallow, but other than that it was fine, so we headed back to the front door.

"The Grandview doesn't look bad in the daylight and from the outside," I said, surveying the building's large windows and pleasant sandstone facade. "It could really be something. A real getaway in the mountains."

"The renovation costs would be out of most people's reach," Gilroy said, "but yeah, it's a nice building in a great spot."

"Juniper Grove owns the land. I wonder why the town never collaborated with Arthur to fix the place up. Paint wouldn't cost much. Paint anything that isn't original wood paneling a soft white or cream color. Instant facelift. Bring in some new furniture, especially to the lobby, put some flower vases around the place."

"You've thought this through."

"Spending a night in the most depressing place I've ever seen might have something to do with that. Have you tried your phone again?"

"No signal. They know we're up here."

"What do you think about Arthur's murder?" I asked. A few months back, when we'd first met—over a dead body in my backyard—Gilroy would have answered that question with an icy stare from his pale blue eyes. But he knew my writer's imagination and my curious nature often got the best of me. If clues presented themselves, I simply *had* to work them out. But more than that, he now respected my opinion on cases. He was the police chief, but I'd proven myself to be a not-too-shabby sleuth.

"I don't think either of the Swansons killed him."

"Really?"

"I'm not writing them off entirely, but they were focused on tearing apart that fireplace using Herbert Purdy's ghost as cover for the noise. I don't see them taking on two jobs—hunting for treasure and killing Mr. Jago. They don't seem sufficiently organized or motivated. All they care about is finding something worth money in the fireplace."

"I see what you mean," I said. "Too much for them to handle. And they had no motive, really. By all accounts Arthur was a good employer."

"They have a nice suite on the third floor. Rent free."

"Trouble is, I can't see why any of them would kill Arthur. What's anyone's motive? Shane benefited from the remote broadcasts on the anniversaries of Purdy's murder. So did Dustin—he's been here before. Maria and Conyer are new to the Grandview broadcasts, but that gives them even less of a motive to murder Arthur."

Gilroy sighed and rubbed the dark stubble on his chin. He looked in need of a good strong cup of coffee. "I need to start doing some digging in town," he said. "I don't think additional interviews are going to get me anywhere."

Feeling the chill—made worse on an empty stomach—I wrapped my arms around my chest. "The killer could be anyone. Everyone except the Swansons were in room 108 just before the banging started. Then Shane and the crew left to record the noise." I threw out my hand. "No, wait. Dustin told Maria and Conyer to record the noise. Everyone assumed it was coming from contracting air ducts, so those two went to the basement, Conyer ahead of Maria."

"Before the others did," Gilroy said, nodding.

He already knew the sequence of events, but I had to go through it again in my mind. I had to say it out loud in order to picture it.

"So Maria and Conyer left while Arthur was still in 108," I went on. "Then after Shane asked how long they had until air time, he and Dustin took off. A minute later, so did Holly and I. Julia says Arthur left right after that. He poured her a cup of coffee, said he had something important to do, and took off."

"And the only people you saw in the basement were Shane and Maria," Gilroy said.

"Right. Maria first, then Shane. I never saw or heard Dustin or Conyer, but they were already back in the room when I got upstairs. Shane and Maria came upstairs with Holly and me. I remember Julia asking if we'd seen Arthur."

"And you didn't notice anything in the library?"

I cringed. "He must have been dead when we walked

past the door on our way back to 108. But you have to step inside the room to see someone sitting in that chair. Which makes me wonder now how Connie saw Arthur."

"She told me she went to the library to get that photo album for Shane so he could talk about it during the show."

"That sounds about right. Shane was asking to see it."

"So at one time or another," Gilroy said, "everyone but you and Holly were separated from the others."

"You're right. Conyer came back with Dustin, but he left with Maria. Dustin left with Shane, but he came back with Conyer. And Shane left with Dustin, but he ended up alone in the basement, just like Maria. Any of them could have run upstairs, killed Arthur, and then gone back to the basement—or to the broadcast room."

Gilroy shoved his hands in his coat pockets, pivoted back to the lobby windows, and stared impassively through them. I knew that expression. His wheels were turning.

"I think the killer asked to meet Arthur in the library," he said after a moment. "This was well planned. Did Connie or Ian make a point of telling you about the banging noises before they began?"

"Connie did. She said they weren't sure what the sounds were, but they were probably the air ducts."

"Leaving open the possibility that they were the work of Herbert Purdy."

"Exactly."

Gilroy returned to that unfocused stare of his. By now I knew enough about how he solved crimes to let him think in peace. I told him I was going to see if I could rustle up some fireplace coffee, then headed back inside.

Holly was wide awake and Julia was valiantly trying to stir herself when I returned to the couch. "Still no sign of the coroner or power company," I said quietly. Underhill was up too, I saw, stretching his legs and arms and gazing longingly at the now-empty coffee carafes. "I'm going to see if Connie and I can make coffee."

"Good idea," Holly said. "I'll come with you."

Ten minutes later, Holly and I had restarted the fire in the fireplace and Ian had set a cast-iron pot on the logs, getting our hot water going. Connie brought a French coffee press and a fresh set of mugs from the kitchen and set them out by the carafes. By now the radio crew was awake. Shane had gone outside to talk to Gilroy, Maria and Dustin were talking about radio commercials, and Conyer, having found a deck of cards in an end-table drawer, had started a game of solitaire.

From what I'd seen of Conyer, his card game was appropriate. He was a solitary man, which I found odd for someone in the very public business of radio, and most of the time he appeared glum and dissatisfied with his life. But maybe it was the hotel that bothered him. Outside of its dark walls, he might have been as bubbly as Shane.

The scene before me was tranquil, almost cozy, but if Gilroy was right, Shane or one of his crew was a murderer. I wasn't ready to erase Connie and Ian from my list of suspects, but I was leaning in that direction.

Find the motive and I'll find the killer, I thought. Was Herbert Purdy's death connected to Arthur's? Did Shane or his crew have any connection to that fifty-year-old murder?

I needed to go back to room 108, to study the photos on my phone and go over in my mind, step by step, the circumstances surrounding Purdy's death. I couldn't put a finger on it, but something was very wrong with that crime scene. More than the pajamas, the single knife wound, and the unmade bed. It was a long shot, but if the two murders were connected, making sense of one might unlock the door to the other.

"Holly, didn't you say you had some pastries in your room?" I asked.

"Want some?" she said. "I wouldn't trust the cream puff after a night in my suitcase, but the donuts and bear claws are okay."

"I need to go to room 108," I replied in a low voice. "Let's say we're getting the pastries so no one follows. Coming, Julia?"

"The things I do," she said, throwing off her blanket.

Holly announced that she had extra pastries in her room—setting the lobby buzzing—and the three of us took off, looking as casual and innocent as possible. When we hit the hall, we quickened our pace.

I glanced at the library door as we sped past, half expecting it to be open, but it remained shut. Near the other end of the hall, room 108's door stood wide open.

I was taken aback by how airy the room seemed in the light of day. The sun, reflecting off the snow, had vanquished the gloom. Julia had noticed, too. When I shut the door behind us, she calmly went to a corner of the room and sat on the chair Arthur had occupied the night before as he ate his eclairs.

"That Herbert Purdy crime scene is such a fake," she said. "Stabbed in his pajamas in a hotel full of strangers. It was staged."

I stared. "You think so too?" I asked.

"Of course I do. I've never heard such nonsense. I might not write mysteries for a living, but I know baloney when I hear it."

"But do you think Purdy's murder is connected to Arthur's?"

Julia pursed her lips, considering my question, then nodded slowly. "Purdy's murder is why we're all here, isn't it?"

CHAPTER 10

"Holly, stand by the door," I said. "You're the killer."

Holly about-faced, stepped over one of the radio crew's cables, and pressed her back to the room's door.

"I'm Herbert Purdy," I went on. "I'm a businessman who just drove from Sterling to the Grandview, on my way to Craig to meet my family."

"It's about a three-hour drive from Sterling," Holly said. "Maybe a little more. I'll bet he put in a full day at work first, and that's why he stopped here instead of going straight through."

"It wasn't a work day," Julia said from her corner chair. "It was a Sunday."

"How do you know?" Holly said.

"While you were down in the basement chasing noises, Arthur told me. He said there weren't many guests that night because it was a Sunday and Sunday was checkout day. Otherwise the hotel would have been fully booked."

"I didn't think you'd talked about it," I said.

"We didn't, really. Thirty seconds while he poured me coffee. For some strange reason, he thought I was interested. I suppose because everyone else is. When he said he had to leave, I said I didn't want to hear any more about the murder. Seeing as I was about to be sitting all by myself in the murder room."

I grinned. "Thank you, Julia. So why did Purdy stop at the Grandview? Connie said he ate dinner at the hotel, so he got here early enough for that."

"It's a convenient cutoff point, isn't it?" Holly said. "From here west, it's all mountain driving. Higher and higher."

"And he wouldn't want to take the mountain roads and passes at night," I said. "Not in January. But he could have driven straight through if he'd left Sterling at, say, seven o'clock in the morning. Wasn't he eager to start his vacation?"

"Why start your vacation on Sunday?" Holly said.

"Connie's the expert," Julia said. "You need to ask her."

I reached for my phone and started flipping through the Purdy crime-scene photos. "All the furniture is in the same place as it was back then," I said. "Different furniture, but the same spots. There's not much choice where to put a bed and dresser in a room this size." I dropped the phone on the bed. "So I arrive at the hotel, eat dinner, talk awhile with the other guests, and go to bed about ten o'clock."

"Sit on the edge of the bed," Holly instructed. "It's ten and you're in your pajamas."

"Right." I sat.

"Are you waiting for someone to visit your room?" Julia asked.

I shook my head. "In my pajamas? Without even a robe? No, I'm not expecting anyone. It's a total surprise when someone comes to the door."

"Then why answer it?" Holly said. "Was there a peephole back then?"

"Good question," I said, going through the crime photos until I came to one of the door. "Yes. Looks like the same peephole, too."

Holly took a quick peek behind her. "And it works. What now?"

"Why do I let you in?" I said. I walked to Holly and pretended to open the door and let her in. "Do I know you? Is that it?"

"Could I be one of the other guests?" Holly said.

"You might have met someone over dinner," Julia said.

"That sounds like a woman," Holly said.

"But remember," I said, "I'm in my pajamas. If it was a planned meeting, I would have stayed dressed."

"Say you let me in," Holly said, taking hold of my shoulders and turning me to face the bed. "We say hello at the door, and I enter. I shut the door behind us, and wherever you're going in your room—the bed, dresser, bathroom— your back is now to the door, and I'm following you into the room."

"And that's when you were stabbed," Julia said, her voice full of conviction.

"Wait a minute," I said. I picked up my phone again, went to the foot of the bed, and faced the headboard. "This is where I'd have to have been standing. Look." I showed Holly the photo of Purdy on the bed. He was face down in the center of it, his head inches from the pillows and his feet and ankles off the mattress. "I've been stabbed, but for some reason I maneuver my way to the end of the bed and fall neatly into the center of the mattress? And then crawl half a foot closer to the pillows? Look, only his feet and ankles are off the bed."

Julia had left her chair, and for the first time she

83

chanced a look at one of the crime-scene photos. "The man almost looks peaceful," she said. "I imagined a terrible scene, but there's hardly any blood."

"I would struggle," I said, "and if I did fall on the bed, I'd be all catty-cornered, with my arms and legs at funny angles."

"You're right," Holly said. "Even if he was stabbed here—and it's very weird to face your bed like that—he still would have twisted his body a little when he was stabbed. Or he would have grabbed at the knife and tried to take it out. He got one stab wound to the back, so I don't think he died instantaneously. Why didn't the killer stab him again?"

"I've wondered that myself," I said. "So was he positioned on the bed after he died? Or just before, maybe?" I whisked through the photos again until I came to one of the bed without Purdy on it. "It's hard to tell with the funky bedspread pattern, but I don't see anything that looks like blood on it. If he struggled with someone on or near the bed, there would have to be blood evidence."

"Or bedspread evidence," Holly. "I mean, come on, there are only a couple wrinkles on that thing. He didn't jerk around at all?"

"Maybe he fell face down on the bed," Julia said. "He didn't get any blood on it that way, and someone pulled him up a few inches so he was closer to the pillows."

"Why?" I asked.

Julia threw her hands in the air. "I haven't the foggiest. Was there blood on the carpet?"

"No," I replied. "Anyway, they tore it up looking for an escape hatch. They might have missed a drop. Can you imagine such shoddy police work?"

"Could Purdy have been killed outside the room?"

Holly asked.

"Walking around in his PJs?" Julia said.

"I keep coming back to him being in his pajamas," I said. "It's ten o'clock, he's tired, he gets undressed—"

"But he doesn't turn down the bed," Holly said.

"No, but other than that . . ." I looked at the photos taken of the bathroom that night. Purdy's, or the hotel's, toothbrush and travel-sized toothpaste were on the sink, along with a used washcloth. "He was ready for bed. He had no intention of leaving his room." I flipped through the photos again. "No robe anywhere."

I heard a popping noise, like a dozen light switches had flicked on at once. The room's ceiling lights went on, and the computer, audio console, surge protectors, and electronic boxes of all sorts came to life, their green and amber lights pulsing.

"The power's back on," Julia said, heaving a contented sigh. "We can have some proper coffee."

I swiped through the photos once more, and as the three of us leaned in, concentrating on them, Dustin pushed through the door and entered the room. I clicked off my phone.

"Hello?" A frown creased his face. With all the expensive radio equipment in the room—equipment he was responsible for—I couldn't blame him for being irritated. "Can I help you ladies with something?"

I decided honesty was the best policy. "I wanted to see the Purdy murder room without a dozen people in it."

Smiling sweetly, Julia said, "We're trying to solve the crime." Her silly-little-old-lady routine had disarmed many an annoyed or suspicious man.

Dustin relaxed, the furrows between his eyes

softening. His hair was still riding high on his head, I noticed. A testament to the strength of his mousse or gel. Even a fitful night on a chair hadn't squashed it much. Noticing other people's hair—something I did on a regular basis—always got me thinking of my own shoulder-length brown hair threaded with gray. I'd avoided mirrors since waking up, but I had no doubt my naturally limp hair was downright stringy this morning.

"You're going to solve a fifty-year-old murder?" Dustin asked.

"Can it hurt to give it a go?" Julia said.

He strode for the desk and yanked open a drawer. "There's no evidence left. You may as well create a version of this room at home." He stopped fiddling in the drawer and looked at me. "Is that what you're doing? Re-creating the murder? Shane said you were good at stuff like that."

"He did?"

"He's read about you in the Juniper Grove paper."

"Don't believe what you read."

Dustin retrieved a set of keys from the drawer, pushed it shut, and flashed a grin. "Radio people know that better than anyone."

"How many remotes have you done at the Grandview with Shane?" I asked.

"This is my fifth."

I sat on the bed. "So what do you think about the Purdy murder?"

Dustin arched a brow. It seemed to me he'd never been asked his opinion before. "I always thought someone made sure it *wasn't* solved. What was the difficulty? You have an isolated hotel, a victim, and a limited number of suspects."

"Like with Arthur," Holly said.

"I guess, yeah. Anyway, it couldn't have been that hard to work out who had it in for Purdy. It had to be one of the guests."

"But how would Purdy and his killer happen to meet at an isolated hotel?" I asked.

"Purdy had a reservation, and his wife knew he'd be staying here overnight."

"But unless one of the guests made a last-minute reservation after finding out Purdy would be—"

"His wife knew," Dustin repeated. "The Purdy family went to Craig every January about the same time. She may have known weeks ahead of time the exact day her husband would be here. Plenty of time to hire someone."

Five trips with Shane to the Grandview had made Dustin a fount of information. "You think his wife hired a hit man?"

Dustin sat on the edge of the desk and crossed his arms. "Every year we go over and over the facts. Shane has a folder of old newspaper articles, and I've read every single one of them multiple times. Not that I believe everything in them. But I don't see another option. One of the guests was a killer for hire."

"What about one of the staff?" Holly asked.

"Everyone on the staff had worked for the Grandview for three years minimum," Dustin said. "Some of them for a decade."

"And killers for hire don't have stable day jobs," I said. Dustin nodded.

"How long were Purdy and his wife married?"

"Twenty-six years."

"After all that time, why would she want him dead?" I asked.

"Word was they were having money troubles and Mrs. Purdy saw herself losing the upper-middle-class life she'd grown to expect. If she divorced him before he lost everything, including his job and house—both of which he was about to lose—she'd get half. If Purdy declared bankruptcy, she'd get nothing. Her kids were adults, so his money would go to her first."

I heard a knock and saw Maria standing just outside the door. "I was sent to ask about the pastries," she said. "Were you storing them in here?"

"We got carried away talking," Holly said, making her way to the door.

"Also, Chief Gilroy says the coroner, the forensics team, and the power company are here," Maria added. "That means the road is passable."

Dustin threw back his head. "It's about time."

"Before you go, Maria," I said, "what do you think about the Purdy murder?"

"You mean the ghost?"

"No, the actual murder."

"All I know is what I've heard Shane say."

"Didn't Shane give you and Conyer a copy of his folder on the case?" Dustin said.

Maria shot a glance down the hall and then looked back to Dustin. "Yeah, but I didn't *read* it."

"You mean you were ill informed?"

Maria smiled wryly. "Did it make a difference?"

Dustin snorted. "Let's get out of here."

It struck me that Maria's fear of Purdy and his ghost, which had been so evident in the basement, had all but evaporated. She was eager to leave the hotel, but she was no longer quaking in fear.

Then again, neither was Julia. Daylight had made all the difference.

"Maria, do you still have that folder?" I asked. "I'd love to take a look at it."

"You can have it," she said. "If I never see the name Purdy again, I'll be a happy woman."

I heard heavy footsteps along the hall floor and a voice call out, "Stop packing, guys."

Maria stared open-mouthed at Dustin.

"Don't pack," Shane said, racing into the room and heading straight for the computer.

Conyer was right behind him, a sour expression on his face. "Shane wants to contact the station," he said.

Shane typed briefly on the keyboard and then hit Send. "I should hear back right away."

Legs planted, hands on her hips, Maria scowled. "I thought we were done. We can't help it if the electricity went out last night."

A minute later, Shane received his answer. "We're staying, folks. They want us on tonight. Live from the Grandview."

CHAPTER 11

On the way home from the Grandview, with Holly at the wheel of her SUV, I sat in the back seat and went over the Purdy folder Maria had given me and browsed my photos of the library—taken after the coroner had removed Arthur's body. Gilroy had allowed me inside, and I'd snapped a quick two dozen photos. The floor, the ceiling, the door, the shelves—every nook and cranny of the place.

I knew from experience that Gilroy didn't like untidy endings. An unsolved murder and all his suspects spending another night at the Grandview? I think if it had been in his power, he would have canceled the remote broadcast set for later. But Connie and Ian had approved it, and with Arthur dead, they acted as the hotel's sole authority.

I was still convinced that the two murders, though fifty years apart, were connected, which was why I had my nose in Maria's Purdy folder on that glittering, cloudless drive out of the foothills. My only proof of a connection, if you could call it proof, was my mistrust of coincidence. I didn't believe in it.

But then, there was also the Purdy photo album, which glowed with the same smudge marks as Arthur's sweater. Someone, perceiving it as a threat, had destroyed its photos in the fireplace. And as Julia had pointed out, Purdy was the reason all of us were at the Grandview. Now I needed to justify my belief that Arthur's death was related to Purdy's with some hard facts.

"Dustin was right about the Purdys' rocky marriage," I said. "If you believe the papers, that is. They were on the verge of a divorce, and the trip to Craig was supposed to be a last-ditch effort to patch up their marriage. Though I don't know why they would bring their adult children along on such a trip."

"Maybe to act as a buffer in case the patch didn't take," Holly said. "I've known couples who have done that."

"Where would Mrs. Purdy hire a hit man?" I said. "A businessman's housewife, born and raised in little Sterling, Colorado. How would she know where to start?"

Julia twisted back to face me. "That's a very good question. I wouldn't know where to hire one, and I've had sufficient reason in my life."

I heard Holly chuckle.

"The town was so small back then, any inquiry along those lines—even as a joke—would have raised eyebrows," I said.

"What if she already knew someone who could do the job?" Holly said. "I'd look into her extended family."

"I need my computer and the Juniper Grove Library." I shut the folder and rested my head on the back of the seat, taking the pressure off my cramped neck muscles. It was one of those Colorado winter days that natives don't like to tell tourists about for fear they would visit, and often. Sky the color of turquoise, the sun outlandishly warm, the air sweet and clear.

"I'm sorry Shane didn't mention your pastries on the radio," I said to Holly, "but maybe he will tonight."

"Are you going to listen?" Holly said.

"I might learn something."

Holly slowed and turned onto Finch Hill Road. I had a date with my computer and corkboard—the same one I used to plot my mysteries. I knew if I could get organized and lay everything out before me, I might see what was niggling at the back of my mind about the two Grandview murders.

Holly pulled in front of Julia's house, and despite her protestations, I helped my next-door neighbor up her walk and porch steps, pulling her luggage behind me. The town hadn't received as much snow as the foothills, but there were still a few unshoveled and cold-crusty inches on the sidewalks and steps. Holly went to her house across the street. My friend had missed out on a golden opportunity at the Grandview. I was tempted to call Shane and ask him to mention her bakery on his show tonight. He and his crew had eaten enough free pastries—it would only be fair.

I got a pot of coffee going, unpacked, and turned on the computer in my office. Next I downloaded the photos from my phone and spread the newspaper articles on the Purdy murder across my desk. I needed to nail down any facts I'd missed.

I drank a cup of strong hazelnut coffee while I clicked through the Purdy crime-scene photos on my monitor. The photo of Herbert Purdy's body, lying neatly in the center of the bed, was a sham. But who had altered the scene? The cops? The killer, trying to protect Mrs. Purdy?

The last newspaper article in the folder hinted that Helena Purdy had something to do with her husband's death. It was a claim she vehemently denied, and the paper was never able to prove a connection between Helena and any of the hotel's guests. Or even her adult children and the guests.

All this despite Helena collecting a hefty insurance payout after Purdy died.

A legend was born when a Denver newspaper gave up on the case and called Purdy's death the "Mystery Murder at the Grandview." At the same time, the nonsense about it being a locked-door killing began. For the journalists involved, drama beat honestly investigating a baffling case.

For the third or fourth time, I studied the Purdy photos. When I came to one of the doorframe—the closeup to show the lock hadn't been jimmied—I saw something new. A neat little blotch of red about a foot above the doorknob. It wasn't a smear, and it didn't have a drip pattern like a spray of blood might. Had any of the wizards at the scene even noticed it? Had they tested it for a fingerprint? My confidence in the Purdy investigation was now so low that I sincerely doubted it.

Hoping Gilroy had made it back to town, I phoned the police station. Travis Turner, the department's newly hired officer from the town of Windsor, Colorado, answered. He expected Gilroy and Underhill soon. When I told him to pass along a question—was it possible for me to get a look at the official report on the Herbert Purdy murder?—Turner surprised me by saying Gilroy had ordered the report from county records this morning. It had been faxed to him from Fort Collins and was sitting on his desk.

I hopped in my car, thinking I'd make it to the station on Main Street about the time Gilroy did, but I had to wait ten nail-biting minutes for him to show up. When he did, he wasn't surprised to see me, and neither was Underhill. Gilroy asked me to follow him, and I shut the door to his office behind me.

"You're here for the Purdy report, aren't you?" he said,

sinking into his chair.

He looked so bone weary, I felt guilty. "How did you know?"

"I saw the look on your face when I was turning the pages in the Purdy photo album."

"Turner said you ordered the report. I know you haven't had a chance to see it yet."

"That's fine. It's an old case," he said, scanning the papers atop his desk. He found the report and slid it toward me. "I hadn't given much credence to the idea that the two murders were connected until you found what was left of the photo album in the fireplace."

Not wanting to put Gilroy in a sticky situation, I didn't even ask to take photos of the five-page report. An official police report, even a very old one, wasn't on the same level as a hotel's photo album and had no business on my personal phone. I read the first page and then glanced up. Gilroy's eyes were closed, his chin was in his hands. I excused myself, poured him a cup of coffee in the lobby, and returned.

"You need this," I said, setting the cup on his desk. "Have you had lunch?"

"Not yet. Thanks." He blew across the cup and took a sip.

"I'm going to pick up something for you and Underhill at Wyatt's Bistro."

"You don't have to do that."

"I know I don't. What do you think of the radio crew spending another night at the hotel?"

"It's not a good idea."

He shut his eyes again and I made quick work of the rest of the report.

94

The thing was full of holes. The police had taken some fingerprints from around the room, but the report made no mention of the smudge above the doorknob. A hotel room was a tricky thing—was a blotch or a smear a clue or simply a result of shoddy housekeeping?—but even I could tell the police had made a halfhearted effort to analyze the scene. They had likely thought they would solve the case through interviews alone. Even so, nothing in the report acknowledged the odd nature of the scene, particularly Purdy's tranquil body position.

A hotel guest across the hall from room 108 had reported hearing a groan just before he heard another sound—a door shutting—but the guest was in bed reading at the time and didn't feel the need to look out his peephole. He thought nothing more of the matter until Purdy's body was found.

The report included a photo of the murder weapon: an everyday, wood-handled kitchen knife, a bit beat-up looking. But no such knife—or any knife at all—was discovered missing from the Grandview's kitchen. Strangely, Purdy had been stabbed with the cutting edge of the knife pointing upward.

Though I'd never held a knife that way in my life, if the killer had acted impulsively, I could imagine him grabbing it the wrong way around. Or maybe a left-hander would do that. Maybe. But it was one more peculiarity I wasn't comfortable with.

In another oversight, no one had checked to see if the knife belonged in any of the guests' homes, but back then, an extensive search like that was beyond either Sterling's or Juniper Grove's budget.

Purdy's murder was destined from the start to go

unsolved.

I slid the report Gilroy's way, quietly closed the door, and took Underhill's lunch order. He was pouring his second cup of coffee as we talked, and he dug into his wallet for twenty dollars to cover lunch.

"What do you think of Arthur Jago's murder, Officer? Any impressions?"

"I don't think he was murdered in the chair."

"I didn't see blood anywhere else."

"Hard to see blood on an oriental rug or in a dark hallway. The crime-scene guys can tell us later."

"I don't think he was killed far from that armchair, though. He was an awfully big guy."

"Dead weight," Underhill said, nodding. "It wouldn't have been easy to carry or drag a man that size to the library."

"Downright impossible, I'd think."

"Unless two people killed him."

"Did you make anything more of the black-light smudges on his shirt?"

"Pastry glaze, wasn't it? He was a sloppy eater."

"But there were no sweeping marks, like this," I said, brushing invisible crumbs from my jacket. "Just small spots. Sloppy eaters brush away the crumbs at some point. And anyway, it didn't look like glaze to me, and Arthur had eclairs. They don't glow under ultraviolet light."

Underhill was a sharp cop. He knew better. But at that moment, like Gilroy, he wasn't firing on all cylinders. I headed off to Wyatt's.

CHAPTER 12

After dropping off Gilroy's and Underhill's sandwiches at the station, I headed back up the sidewalk to see how Holly was doing after our sleepless night at the Grandview. Early afternoon was a slower time at the bakery, so Peter handled the counter as Holly and I took a break in the back. She said she had a new cream puff recipe she was trying, and the first of the new puffs were about to come out of the oven. I wasn't about to pass that up.

"The pastry is chocolate and the cream is almond flavored," she said, her eye on the oven timer. "It may be overkill." When the timer dinged, she removed a tray, set it to cool on a stainless island, left the oven door open until the temperature dropped just so, and then slid a tray of scones onto the rack. Then, in a waltz-like movement, she plucked a ceramic bowl from a refrigerator, grabbed a carton of heavy cream, and wheeled back to the island.

"I'm surprised you're able to function today," I said, admiring her ability to multitask.

"Three mugs of coffee," she replied.

"What else have you got baking?" I glanced about, trying to control an urge to sample one of the chocolate puffs before Holly had a chance to make the cream filling.

"Just the scones."

In answer to my quizzical look, she set down the carton of cream and said, "See that triple-deck oven over there?" She jabbed a thumb over her shoulder. "It's broken, and it can't be fixed. All it's good for is the trash heap."

"When did that happen?"

"Ten days ago. We've been told by two separate repairmen that it can't be fixed. Thank goodness it didn't happen over Christmas or our doors would be shut right now. That's our main oven."

"Can you get a new one?"

"We have to—we have no choice. It was only six months out of warranty. *Six months*."

"They're expensive, aren't they?"

"Royally. We'll have to go into major debt, and you know how I hate that. We had most of this equipment paid off."

No wonder Holly had thought of her missed opportunity when she saw Arthur's body. A major purchase—I guessed at least ten thousand dollars—weighed on her, and with her benefactor gone, that purchase would put her in a financial predicament.

"Holly's Sweets is getting so popular—maybe it won't take long to pay it off."

Holly's mouth was set in a firm line. My optimism wasn't helping. "Peter and I go shopping for a new oven next week. Our lives and our credit card in hand. We paid off the small charges on the card today and we're waiting for the payment to show up before we can charge it again. We've become slaves to the bakery, and that was never my intention."

When I'd first met Holly, I thought she possessed a naturally cheerful spirit. I thought she was one of those lucky souls to whom happiness came naturally. Later, I realized she had to work at her cheerfulness—like most of us. And she did work at it. To see her so uncommonly dejected disturbed me. I resolved to call Shane at the Grandview as soon as I got home. He was going to rave about Holly's Sweets like he'd never raved about anything else or I'd pay him an unpleasant visit at the hotel.

"How about coffee at my house after you and Peter eat dinner?" I said. "I'm inviting Julia. A nice fire in the fireplace, relaxing small talk, friends waiting on you hand and foot?"

"I'd prefer a meeting of the Juniper Grove Mystery Gang."

"Are you up to it?"

"Absolutely, I am. It'll take my mind off this . . . this . . . everything going wrong at once. As a matter of fact," she said, anxiously twisting her wedding ring, "I was thinking of dropping pastries off at the Grandview in two or three hours. Feel like going with me?"

I hesitated, but only out of surprise. I was sure Holly never wanted to see the inside of the Grandview again. But it wasn't a bad idea—bringing the crew more scrumptious pastries—and it would give me a chance to examine the library without feeling rushed or intrusive.

"Sure, I'll go with you. Then we can head back to my place for coffee."

Holly smiled. "It'll be late for me. How about cocoa instead of coffee?"

"You got it."

"Now help me make the almond-flavored filling. You're my guinea pig."

After I gave my official seal of approval to the new cream puff—by eating an entire one—I headed back to my car, but along the way, I glanced through the window of Wyatt's Bistro and saw Shane and his crew chatting over a late lunch. Actually, Shane was doing the chatting. His crew looked as morose as Holly had a few minutes earlier, and the three of them sat silently, chewing like tired and unhappy cows. Now was my chance to talk to Shane about Holly's pastries.

I pasted a smile on my face as I strode to their table. "I didn't expect to see you all down here."

"Well, hey there," Shane said. "We thought we'd take a break, and that police officer—I forget his name. Tall, grumbling guy who came with the chief."

"Underhill."

"Underhill said Wyatt's was tasty. Pull up a chair."

Conyer shot a sidelong look at Maria. I had the distinct feeling I wasn't welcome.

"So you're spending another night at the Grandview," I said. Not a brilliant observation, but it was a conversational starting point.

"We're wondering if Purdy's ghost walks the halls the day *after* his murder," Shane said.

"It doesn't bother you to stay there another night, with all that's happened?" I said.

"Yeesss," Maria said, elongating the word as though fools like me needed to have the obvious made plain. She wore the same blue headband she had at the hotel, and in her anticipation of another miserable night at the Grandview, she tugged at it as she had in the basement.

Conyer peered at me over the top of his glasses. "For all we know, we're safer tonight than we were last night."

"Ouch," Shane said. "Manners."

100

Conyer's remark called for bluntness. "Chances are, you're in every bit as much danger tonight as last night," I said. "Probably more."

Maria frowned and pulled in her chin. "You mean Ian and Connie Swanson? Tell me that's what you mean, 'cause the four of us have been working together almost a year, and I trust everybody at this table."

Intrigued, Shane leaned my way and crossed his arms on the table. "You're the detective, Rachel. Should we be worried about each other?"

If you're not worried now, you never will be, I wanted to say. Instead, I shrugged. "Someone killed Arthur, and the police haven't arrested a suspect. I think you should be careful. Arthur was taken by surprise. He trusted whoever killed him."

"How do you know?" Shane said.

"He was a big guy. If he'd known he was about to be killed, he would have fought back, and no one at this table is strong enough to have taken him head on. Whoever killed Arthur trapped him in some way, and he died shortly after, unable to fight back."

"But why would one of us kill him? I liked the guy."

I couldn't help but notice how swiftly Shane had segued from *us* to *I*, leaving the others without alibis based on affection. "Did you know him before you started doing remotes at the Grandview?"

"I met him a few months before our first remote, a little over five years ago. He was a fan of the show. We struck up a conversation, and he suggested doing a show at the hotel on Purdy's anniversary. The station thought it was a super idea, and since I'm a ghost buff, I did too."

"Are you all ghost buffs?" I asked, looking from

Dustin to Conyer and Maria.

"I hate ghosts," Maria said. "They're idiotic."

"You wound me, Maria," Shane said, clutching his chest.

"They're a way for unscrupulous people to make money off of gullible people."

Shane made an exaggerated gasping sound.

"And thanks to ghosts, I had to creep around a dank basement in the dark."

"Speaking of basements," I said. I had them all together. It was time for a little investigating, even if they took offense at my questions. And they would. "Where was everyone when we went down there to check out the banging noise?"

"Searching for the source," Dustin said. "I followed one of the ducts from near the stairs to a wall on the other side of the building. What a fraud that turned out to be."

"I only saw Maria and Shane down there," I said. "Where were you, Conyer?"

Conyer gave his sliding glasses a shove up his nose. "I was the first one down there—by myself, since Maria had to have a flashlight."

"I was right to wait for a flashlight," Maria said. "I could've broken my neck on the stairs or walked into a wall."

"I made it down all right," Conyer said. "And carrying a recorder too. It wasn't totally black. There were a few bulbs in the ceiling."

"No, Maria's right," Dustin argued. "I wish I'd taken a flashlight. I tripped over—I don't know what it was—when I was down there. I couldn't see. And what a *smell*."

"I thought I'd gag," Maria said. "It stunk like an old sock."

"Believe me, I've smelled better socks," Conyer said with a laugh.

While his crew talked, Shane watched them, his head cocked, his eyes flitting from one co-worker to another. Something was troubling him. A new and disturbing thought had risen to the surface of his mind. I saw it in his expression. Did his memories of that night differ?

Shane turned to me. "Herbert Purdy was taken by surprise too, wasn't he?"

"And just like that, we're back on Purdy," Dustin said. Maria and Conyer chuckled.

"That's my guess," I replied.

"But by definition, anyone stabbed in the back has been taken by surprise," Dustin said.

Shane's eye narrowed. "Am I the only one who thinks it's weird that both Herbert Purdy and Arthur Jago were stabbed in the back on the same date? That's too much of a coincidence to be a coincidence."

"You're not the only one," Conyer said. "I pointed that out. Remember? We were—"

Dustin cut him off. "All you said was there were similarities."

"Why is it a coincidence?" Maria asked. "Death by knife is common."

"True," Conyer said. "Otherwise you're saying any knife murder where the victim is stabbed in the back is connected to the Purdy murder."

I shook my head. "It's more than the knife. It's the location, it's the date, it's the apparent lack of struggle and blood evidence at the murder scenes—so much so that we're not really sure of the exact places Purdy and Arthur were killed."

103

Shane gaped, and I realized I'd said too much.

"Wait a minute," he argued. "Purdy was killed in room 108. That's why we do the remote there every year."

I rushed to reassure him that his knowledge of the case wasn't completely illusory. "He was probably killed somewhere in the room. But I'm not convinced he was attacked on or near the bed."

"Didn't they check the room for blood?" he said.

"Not very carefully, in my opinion."

"Are you saying he was killed, say, in the bathroom or the hall?"

"He might have been stabbed the second he turned his back after opening the door." I omitted mention of the red smudge above the doorknob and the ear-witness's report of a loud sigh coming from the hall.

Her lips pursed in agitation, Maria said, "But Arthur was killed in the library. Connie found him."

"Connie found his *body*," I corrected.

"Thus the library is not necessarily the murder scene," Shane said. "But as you said, Arthur was a big guy. Who could move him?"

"Maybe he moved himself."

Shane was gaping again. "He walked?"

And again I shrugged. Suddenly I wanted the conversation to end. Shane had a fascination for the Purdy case that wasn't wholly healthy, and it dawned on me that I was telling four murder suspects too much about Arthur's death. I was becoming as gabby as Officer Underhill, and no good could come from that.

I rose and pushed my chair under the table. "Shane, would you mind talking about Holly's pastries tonight? She missed out last night. Arthur was her business angel and, well, she's in a bit of a bind now. Her main and very expensive oven died."

"Sure thing. Those were some of the best bear claws I've ever had, and I've traveled a lot. Was she paid for all those pastries?"

"I don't think so. I believe part of the payment was going to be the on-air promotion."

"That's not fair, is it?" Shane said. "I'll make it up. Promise."

"Best cinnamon-honey rolls ever," Conyer said. He nudged Maria. "Miss Vitamin here missed out."

"Hey, I had a chocolate croissant, remember? Man, it was good. Tell Holly I said that, okay?"

"You just tell her to listen tonight," Shane said. "She's in for a pleasant surprise."

"We're spending another night at Murder Hotel," Conyer said. "I have a feeling we're *all* in for a surprise."

CHAPTER 13

Any one of Shane's colleagues could have killed Arthur. They'd all had the opportunity. As I left Wyatt's Bistro, I wondered if Shane had come to that realization as he listened to his crew talk about their adventures in the hotel's basement. Did he suspect, as I did, that one of them was a killer?

Not that I'd totally dismissed Shane from my list of suspects. His affable nature aside, he was an ambitious man who put his work first. If Arthur had suggested they end the Purdy broadcasts, how would he have reacted? The Swansons claimed they had tried to talk Arthur into rebranding the hotel as a pleasant mountain getaway. What if they had succeeded?

All I knew about Shane's crew was what I had observed at the hotel. They seemed incapable of murder. They were unwilling participants in a remote broadcast from a creepy hotel. But more than that, none of them seemed to have a motive.

But someone did have a motive. It was more important than ever to find out *why* Arthur was killed.

I climbed into my Forester and rang the Swansons on my cell. A minute later, I had a new piece of the puzzle. In his will, Arthur Jago had left the hotel to his brother,

Raymond. He'd told the Swansons about the will last fall. He wanted them to rest assured that if something happened to him, they were to be kept on as managers for at least one year after his death. After that, Raymond could do what he wished, including sell the hotel.

It was Raymond who had introduced Arthur to Shane Rooney and put a bug in Arthur's ear about a remote broadcast, Connie said. Raymond, a wealthy businessman who lived in Denver, owned half the Fort Collins radio station where Shane worked and had an interest in the Purdy mystery going unsolved. At least once a year, during the Purdy remote, advertisers were willing to pay exorbitant rates for commercials.

I drove home for a late lunch and a quick visit with Julia. I thought someone should know Holly and I intended to take more pastries to the radio crew, and I wasn't about to tell Gilroy. Julia poured me a cup of boiling water, plopped a teabag in it, and led me into her living room, where we seated ourselves in her favorite chairs, one on either side of the large window overlooking her front porch. It was the sentry spot from which she observed the neighborhood goings-on.

"I can't believe you're going back to that awful place after all that happened," she said. "You know what Chief Gilroy would say."

How often did she use that one me? *What would Chief Gilroy say?* "Listen, Julia, it makes good sense for Holly to drop off pastries. She's going to go whether or not I do, and I'd rather she didn't go alone." When I told Julia about Holly's very broken and very expensive triple-deck oven, and reminded her that last night was a financial loss for her, she relented.

"But once you two have dropped off the food, turn around and get out of there pronto."

"After I take a peek at the library."

Julia gave me a withering look.

"I'm missing something obvious, Julia. I have that feeling. I'll know what it is when I see the library again, but I need to see it."

"You do realize Juniper Grove is blessed with a very competent police chief, don't you?"

I took a long drink of tea. "I can't help it. I'm a mystery writer and it's in my blood."

"This is not a novel, Rachel. This is real life. And real death."

"I see clues and I need to put them together and solve the puzzle. And Gilroy knows that."

Julia started twirling a strand of gray hair around her finger. I recognized the expression on her face. She didn't want to be left out of the adventure, to have to hear secondhand the exciting things that had happened. "The only puzzle is *which* of those people murdered Arthur Jago," she said. "You know one of them did."

"I don't think the Swansons killed Arthur, and neither does Gilroy."

"That's something, I suppose. Of course, the Swansons could be murdered too, just like Arthur. In fact, they could be dead right now."

"With the radio people there? They're not all killers, Julia, and I think Arthur was the only target. Come with us. You know you want to solve the puzzle. I can see it in your face."

"If I go with you and something happens, there'll be no one left alive to tell Chief Gilroy the foolishness we've been up to."

"If he finds our bodies up there, he'll figure it out soon enough."

Julia waved her hand impatiently. "You know I can't say no. I hate being left behind."

"I promise we'll all stick together. We'll drop the pastries off, go to the library, then come straight to my house and listen to the show. Shane promised to rave about Holly's bakery."

"I must be out of my mind. We all are."

"You don't believe in ghosts, do you?"

"I believe in bad people, Rachel. I've seen my fair share."

Realizing she was genuinely worried and not simply chiding me in her Julia Foster way, I tried to reassure her that we would be careful. "We'll keep our eyes open and get out quickly, I promise you. We'll never be alone with any of them."

"Shane looks strong enough to fight off all three of us at once," she said.

"Yeah, but he likes you. That's why he calls you Miss Julia."

"Stop," she said, biting back a grin. Two seconds later, her face fell. "Arthur never saw it coming, did he? You and Holly said he had a shocked expression on his face when he died. Someone took advantage of his trust."

"I know that, but the only advantage-taking tonight will be Holly taking advantage of an opportunity she desperately needs." I scooted to the edge of my seat and drank a last sip of tea.

"Could Holly and Peter lose the bakery?" Julia asked.

With my attention focused on two murder cases, the

possibility that the Kavanaghs might lose Holly's Sweets hadn't entered my mind. "If they don't quickly make back the money they have to spend on a new oven, it's possible. They're using their credit card, and the interest on that has to be outrageous. But we're not going to let that happen. People will be driving to Holly's Sweets from all over northern Colorado after they listen to Shane tonight."

Two hours later, with the sun setting behind the foothills, the three of us drove to the Grandview with thirty-two assorted pastries in pink boxes. Probably more than the Swansons and radio crew could eat in one night—even Conyer—but Holly wanted to err on the side of too many. Peter stayed behind to close the bakery, but he wasn't happy about Holly heading to Murder Hotel again. He'd said something about putting his foot down and taking the pastries himself, but Holly told him she could get more on-air accolades out of Shane herself. He knew her, not Peter.

This time we parked right in front of the hotel's main door. Connie Swanson greeted us there and walked with us to the kitchen, where Ian was making sandwiches for the evening.

"Are those pastries just for the crew?" he asked.

"They're for everyone," Holly said. "Though I want to save at least two of each for the radio guys. I'm hoping to get their endorsement."

Connie brought out napkins and platters and set them next to the boxes. "I was wondering, Holly. Would your bakery be interested in catering special events? Like Easter, the Fourth of July, weddings, conferences?"

I explained to Holly that Arthur's brother Raymond now owned the hotel, and that the Grandview would remain a hotel for at least a year.

"Ian and I are good cooks," Connie said, "but when it comes to baking—"

"We stink," Ian finished. "Connie and I were talking about it this afternoon. An Easter buffet, things like that. It would be a tall order."

"And we'd have to talk Raymond Jago into it," Connie said, "but we thought if we could show him that this could be a destination hotel, he might keep us on past one year."

Holly didn't hesitate. "I'd love to. I do savory baked goods too. Spinach and ham croissants, that kind of thing. But I could bring both—whatever you want."

"Fabulous!" Connie said. "You know, I think if Arthur had lived, he would have changed this place. He never said so explicitly, but I think he was growing bored with the whole Purdy ghost thing."

You weren't bored with it, I wanted to say. I was thinking of adding my two contrary cents, but I clamped my mouth shut, not wanting to spoil Holly's possible business relationship with the Swansons. It still irked me that they had driven everyone crazy with their late-night noise-making. "Where are Shane and his crew?" I asked.

"In room 108," she replied.

Julia heaved a sigh.

"Would you mind if we took a quick look at the library?" I asked, tossing my head in that direction.

Connie and Ian exchanged sidelong glances. "If you really want to," Connie said. "The police said we could use it again. I shut the door, but it's not locked."

"Now we have two ghosts in this hotel," Ian said as he put away the mustard and mayo.

"Stop it, Ian," Connie said.

111

"One of these days we're going to get a normal job," he groused.

"In the meantime, we still have to sleep here, so no more ghost talk."

"Are there other guests tonight?" I asked. "If I remember right, Arthur said the hotel was closed to guests last night only, for the show."

"We had six cancellations this morning," Connie said. She chewed on the inside of her lower lip. "Three couples, two families with small children, and a single. No one has canceled yet for tomorrow, but we'll see."

"Give it time," Holly said. "It's been less than twenty-four hours since Arthur died. People will start coming back."

"That's what I keep telling myself," Connie said. "I guess we should be grateful that Raymond won't toss us out in two weeks, and I don't think he knows anything about us digging up the fireplace. Chief Gilroy decided to let us off the hook."

Holly, Julia, and I made our way through the lobby to the library. For some silly reason, I knocked on the door before opening it. Then I flicked on the light switch and stepped inside.

"What are you looking for?" Holly asked.

"I wish I knew. I've never felt so strongly about something with such little evidence to back up my feelings." I walked around to the armchair in which Arthur's body had been found and then walked back to the door. "I wonder if the crime-scene evidence has come back yet." I bent forward and examined the oriental rug. "Do either of you see blood anywhere?"

"Oh my," Julia said, taking a tentative step into the library. "If only murders didn't have blood. I wouldn't mind half so much."

Holly cast her eyes over the carpet. "There are stains on it, but it's almost impossible to tell what they are."

I took a closer look at the chair and found what appeared to be drops of blood where the back met the seat. Exactly where you'd expect it if Arthur, his heartbeat slowed to a crawl, had taken his dying breaths in the chair.

I went back and stood in the open doorway. If Arthur had been stabbed on the library threshold, why walk to the armchair? I moved to the shelves opposite the armchair and again tried to imagine what had happened. "This library is small and stuffed with furniture," I said. "If someone came up behind me in this small space, I'd feel awkward. I don't even know how they'd do it without the hairs on the back of my neck standing up. I wonder if he was standing in the doorway when he was attacked."

Three short strides and I was back at the door. "It's too small," I said, shaking my head. I inspected the door for a smudge of blood, like I'd seen above the doorknob on room 108. Nothing. Then I checked the doorframe near the knob. Again, nothing. But on the doorframe on the opposite side of the door, I noticed a strange indentation about an inch and a half wide.

"What is it?" Holly said.

"This is such an old hotel," I said, my frustration and impatience growing. "I don't know what I'm looking at or when it was put there. No wonder the Purdy murder was never solved."

My mind flitted from Arthur to Purdy and back again. From the Purdy murder room to the library. From wood-handled knife to wood-handled knife. From drops of blood in an armchair to a smudge of blood above a doorknob.

113

"Come with me," I said.

I raced down the hall for room 108, Holly and Julia on my heels.

CHAPTER 14

"Well, how about that," Shane said. "I had no idea you ladies were here."

"I brought more pastries," Holly said, giving me a private nudge with her elbow. "They're in the kitchen." She wanted to remind me what she had come for, to tell me to tread lightly with my sleuthing. I understood.

"Seeing as how last night was so difficult," I said, "Holly thought you could use some pick-me-ups."

"You didn't have to do that," Shane said. "Not that I mind. But I was going to talk about your bakery anyway. Now that you're here, you're all welcome to stay and listen."

"Thank you, but I have to get back," Holly said. "*We* have to get back."

"I'll go get the pastries," Conyer said, already racing out the door. I was betting he'd devour at least one cinnamon-honey roll before he made it back to the room.

"I just needed to, sort of . . . ," I said vaguely, pointing at the room's door.

"Rachel Stowe," Shane said with a sly grin, "you're still investigating the Purdy murder."

"It's an intriguing case," I said as evasively as possible.

"You should stay for the show and talk about it," Maria said, pushing past Dustin into the room.

115

"No, we have to leave," Julia said.

"Where have you been?" Dustin asked Maria.

Maria glared at him. "Do I have no privacy? I'm the only woman here."

"That's a fantastic idea," Shane said. "Stay, Rachel. We can bounce ideas off each other on the air."

Dustin looked bewildered. "I'll never understand the fascination. Whoever killed Purdy is probably dead now. It's not like you can see justice done."

"His kids are probably still alive," Holly said. "They'd want to know what happened."

"I'll tell you the fascination," Shane said. "It's trying to solve an unsolvable crime."

"What if someone *has* solved it?" I said.

Shane and his crew froze.

"I didn't say *I* solved it," I quickly added.

Shane laughed and slapped his leg. "Oh, yes you did. You just did. You can't drop that bombshell and take off. Now you *have* to stay. You sit yourself down and talk to my audience." He pointed his long forefinger at me. "I knew the moment you heard the facts of the case you saw something others didn't."

"So did you, Shane," I said. "Only in all these years, you've never let on."

From the corner of my eye I saw Holly and Julia, utterly confused, glance from me to Shane.

"Telling wouldn't be in my own best interest, would it?" he said. "Or the station's."

"But things have changed. Arthur was murdered."

"Yes, his death changes things. Though I'm still not positive of my conclusion. Are you?"

"What is going on?" Holly said.

116

"I'm not positive," I said. "Yet. But we're not the only two who think they know what happened, are we?"

"Seriously, you guys," Holly said. "This is royally frustrating. What are you talking about?"

Conversation stopped when Conyer and Connie entered the room with two platters full of pastries. Behind them, Ian carried a tray bearing a pot of coffee and four cups. Ian positioned the tray on the bureau, and Conyer and Connie set the platters on the bed, Conyer quickly snagging a cinnamon-honey roll for himself.

"Connie, can I borrow a knife from your kitchen?" I asked.

Understandably, she was horrified.

"What on earth for?" Ian said.

"I want to test a theory."

Shane stood. "Just you and me, Rachel."

"Holly and Julia come too," I said.

"Agreed."

"Goodness," Julia said. "This is suspenseful."

"You guys stay here," Shane said to his crew as he exited the room. Holly, Julia, and I trailed behind him, heading for the kitchen.

"Are knives a good idea?" Connie called out. "Considering?"

I glanced over my shoulder. Ian. Connie, and the others had stayed behind in room 108, which was just as well. I didn't want to tip my hand on what I knew—or thought I knew—and neither did Shane, by the looks of it.

In the kitchen I found a wood-handled paring knife and decided it would do. "What do you know about Purdy's life?" I asked Shane.

"Just what I read in the newspaper articles I collected.

117

Maria told me she gave you the folder on the case. I'm afraid that's the extent of my knowledge. I've never met anyone who knew him personally."

"Do you know the cutting edge of the knife that killed him was facing upward?"

Shane's eyes narrowed. He looked behind him, found another knife, and held it cutting edge up.

Julia took several steps back.

"I have no intention of hurting anyone, Miss Julia," Shane said. "I just want to see . . ." He looked at the blade in his hand. "Who holds a knife like this? Cutting vegetables or stabbing someone—your natural inclination is to hold it like this." He turned the cutting edge down.

"That's the problem." I said. "There was no natural inclination here. It was well thought out, and not at all what it appeared to be. It's very simple, really. Let's go to a room on the second floor, away from prying eyes."

My friends were a little reluctant, but they followed us up the room-service stairs to the first room on the second floor. When we got to the room, I opened the door and the four of us stepped inside.

"A witness heard a groan, and then a moment later, a door shut," I said. "It must have been Purdy's door he heard."

"I never read that," Shane said.

"It was in the official police report."

"How did you find—"

"A friend," I said.

"You've had an unfair advantage."

"I suppose I have. So tell me, what killer would have knocked on the door—knowing other guests could look out their peephole—and then stabbed Purdy? The groan the witness heard was Purdy being stabbed, I'm sure of it. And the sound of the door closing was Purdy shutting his own door."

Shane grinned. "Like minds," he said.

"Everyone gets this but me," Holly said.

"Not just you," Julia said. "Will you two please spill it?"

"Purdy was about to lose everything," I said. "Twenty-six years of marriage and a good job about to go down the drain. So instead of joining his wife and kids in Craig, trying to resuscitate his marriage, he spends a night at an isolated hotel. That's the first oddity. He gets into his pajamas but doesn't get into bed, and a stranger comes to the door and kills him without a struggle. Does any of that make sense?" I shut the door most of the way. Next I turned the cutting edge of my knife upward, stuck the handle between the frame and the hinge side of the door, and closed the door as much as the handle would allow. Then I let go of the knife and stepped back.

"And there it is," Shane said. He reached out to jiggle the blade, but it barely budged. "Firm enough to do the job, but not stuck in there. It would pop out when he walked forward."

"Are you kidding me?" Holly said.

"Purdy bought a knife, or stole it from a restaurant, and brought it with him to the hotel," I said. "That night, he got into his pajamas, jammed it in his own door, and backed into it."

"You're joking," Julia exclaimed. "He wasn't murdered?"

Shane rubbed his chin in wonder. "I have puzzled over this for *years*. I came to the same conclusion, but no one else ever talked about the possibility that Purdy killed himself. I thought I must be wrong."

"Purdy couldn't help but groan when he backed into the knife," I went on. "He backed up hard. He had to in order for his plan to work. That's what the witness heard. And with the knife in his back, he walked forward and then reached back and shut the door all the way. The witness heard that too. I think Purdy reflexively touched his back, getting blood on his fingers, and when he shut the door, he left a smudge of blood above the doorknob."

"I didn't know about a smudge either," Shane said. "Was it in the official report?"

"The police never mentioned it or tested it. I saw it in one of the photos in the album the Swansons put in the library."

"So after Purdy did this, he went to lie down on his bed," Holly said. "That's why there didn't appear to be a struggle. There *wasn't* one. But why was he wearing pajamas?"

Shane spread his hands. "With insurance money involved, he didn't want to make it easy on the police, so he threw red herrings at them. If they declared his death a suicide, no money."

I nodded. "That's right. There's never a payout for suicide."

"But even if he and his wife were divorcing, he still cared about his family, his kids," Shane said.

Holly threw back her head. "In fifty years no one else has figured this out?"

"Someone else figured it out," I said, looking to Shane. "Someone outside this room."

"Now hold on," he said. "You're talking about people

I work with. Friends. Downstairs stuffing their faces with bear claws. Do they look like killers to you?"

"One of them noticed that smudge of blood in the photo—among a dozen other weird things about the crime scene—and burned the album in the fireplace last night so no one else could see it."

"What about the Swansons? Aren't they likely candidates?" Shane said.

"Why would the Swansons put the album together, talk to everyone about it, and then burn it?"

Shane said nothing for a moment, and it seemed to me he was searching for ways to refute my words and exonerate his crew. He liked them, and contemplating the possibility that one of them was a murderer was a painful exercise. "But think about this," he said. "What difference does that photo album make? Purdy died fifty years ago. Why burn the photo-album proof of how he died? I don't see what it has to do with Arthur's murder. The worst you can say is that someone in my crew destroyed hotel property."

"Come with me," I said, exiting the room.

"Lead on," Shane said.

"Where are we going now?" Julia said.

I made my way back down the service stairs, strode through the kitchen and lobby, and went back to the library. I half expected to see someone waiting for us in the lobby or hall, but there was no one. I shut the library door most of the way and directed everyone's attention to the odd indentation I'd seen earlier. "About an inch and a half wide," I said. "If memory serves, it's about the width of the wood-handled knife used to stab Arthur."

"My, my, my," Shane said, leaning in close. "This is not good."

"There may have been blood here. Cleaned up to the naked eye but still detectable to the forensics team. Results haven't come back yet."

"Rachel, are you saying Arthur killed himself the same way Purdy did?" Julia asked.

"No."

Shane looked up slowly.

"I'm saying that one of Shane's crew figured out the Purdy puzzle, lured Arthur to the library with the promise of an answer to the mystery, and demonstrated that answer to Arthur. His back was probably a couple inches from the knife. He had no idea what was about to happen."

Shane stood bolt straight. "They all separated when they went down to the basement. And they came back up separately."

"That's the only time it could have happened," I said. "Going down or coming back up."

"Well, this is a bad pickle," Shane said, giving his chin another rub. "I'm on air in an hour. I have no choice but to work with them." His voice dropped and took on a serious tone. "I'm literally not going to be able to turn my back on my own crew."

"I need to call Chief Gilroy," I said, "and you need to talk to your station and cancel the show." I spoke with as much certitude and authority as I could gather, hoping to convince Shane.

"That can't happen," he answered. "Dead air two nights in a row—it's not possible."

"Shane, you want to talk about dead air? Your life is at stake."

"You don't cancel a show in this business. Advertisers are already breathing down our necks because of last night."

A loud voice sounded from somewhere down the hall.

"That's Dustin," Shane said, taking hold of the doorknob. "He needs a sound check."

"Wait just a second," I said. "You know Dustin, Maria, and Conyer better than anyone. Which one of them would have a reason to kill Arthur?"

"None of them, for crying out loud," Shane said, jamming his fingers into his curls. "When I think about it, none of them. That's the thing. That's why I think I'll be okay doing the show. I'll be all right. They're good people."

"Arthur felt safe too," I said. I looked into his eyes, letting that sink in before I went on. "Promise me you won't be alone in the room with just one of them. Make sure at least two of your crew are with you at all times."

"That's easy enough," he said, relaxing his posture a bit. "It's all hands on deck when we're on air, and no one's going to kill me while we're broadcasting."

"Then watch yourself before and after you're on the air."

As Shane hurried down the hall to finish preparations for his show, I phoned Gilroy from the hotel's land line, which thankfully was working again. He wasn't happy when he learned where I was.

CHAPTER 15

Gilroy instructed me in no uncertain terms to leave the Grandview in Holly's SUV. Now. We weren't to wait for him to arrive. The tone of his voice seesawed between angry and anxious, tending toward the angry end of the scale. I had a feeling that after a long respite, I was about to hear the word "meddling" again.

The three of us walked out of the Grandview, climbed into the SUV, and locked the doors. But when Holly put her key in the ignition to get the heat going, nothing happened. No sputtering, no clicking, nothing. There were lights on the dashboard, but no life in the engine.

"It can't be the battery," I said. "It wouldn't just die like that."

Holly agreed. "The battery was fine when we got here, and it's only been fifteen minutes."

"I wonder if someone tampered with it," I said.

"Thank you very much for bringing up that possibility," Julia said, leaning forward from the back seat. "It hadn't crossed my mind until this moment."

"Pop open the hood lock so I can take a look," I said.

When I lifted the hood, even I could tell what the problem was. We were in trouble. I let the hood fall and climbed back into my seat. "Someone opened your fuse box.

The top is missing and it looks like a few fuses were yanked out."

Holly's jaw dropped. "Why? What reason would they have for making sure we can't leave?"

"Maybe it was just malicious," I said, grasping at straws. It was a ridiculous answer, but I wanted to say something calming. Our cell phones didn't work and it wasn't smart to try to walk out of the foothills on a January night. We were stuck. Julia, who was certain we'd be attacked from behind at any moment, kept glancing out the rear window, making me even more nervous.

"Gilroy will be here any minute now," I said.

"I have half a mind to march in there and tell them all what-for," Julia said. "Scaring us like this. And Holly brings them free pastries—two nights in a row, mind you—and how do they reward her? By vandalizing her car."

"Someone wants us to stay here," Holly said. "That's what scares me."

"I spent too much time on the Purdy case," I said. "I just had to prove I could solve the unsolvable puzzle. But I haven't got the first clue why Arthur was murdered. And now we're . . . we're . . ."

"Sitting ducks?" Holly offered.

"I was going to say in trouble. And so is Shane."

Julia leaned forward again. "Solving the Purdy case helped with Arthur's murder. Now we know how he died and why the photo album was burned. Instead of bemoaning our situation, let's put our heads together, shall we? I plan on living a little longer."

I had to grin. "Who are you, and what have you done with Julia?" Though sometimes easily spooked, my sweet neighbor also, paradoxically, had a knack for cutting to the heart of things—and at times she possessed a fearlessness I envied.

"Nonsense," Julia said, poking me in the shoulder. "Now what do we know about the case?"

"Arthur was killed by someone going down to or coming out of the basement in search of that noise," I said. "And I think, though I can't prove it, that the killer was showing Arthur how Purdy died. I think Arthur was lured to the library with the promise that he would finally learn the secret to Purdy's so-called murder."

"That means the killer set up a meeting before Connie and Ian started banging away on that third-floor fireplace," Holly said.

"Arthur did rush out of the room," Julia said. "Thinking back on it, he was very excited."

"So . . ." I closed my eyes, imagining the scene in the library. "Arthur went to the library. Maybe the killer was already waiting for him. The door might have been shut. I don't remember if it was, and I don't think anyone else noticed."

"I didn't," Holly said.

"The killer tells Arthur he has to *show* him, not tell him, how Purdy died," I continued.

"And Arthur is very excited and willing," Holly said. "He's been trying to work out this mystery since he was a twelve-year-old boy."

I opened my eyes. "The killer puts the knife in the door, positions Arthur close to it, and pushes."

"Oh, dear," Julia said. "The poor man."

"No wonder he had that look on his face," Holly said.

"Maybe the killer put his hands—no, his fingers—on Arthur's chest before he pushed. Gently. Just his fingers so

Arthur wouldn't be frightened." My thoughts were racing. The scene played over and over in my mind. "Arthur was a big man, and he if he'd known he was about to be pushed into a knife, he would have fought back. Successfully. But the knife was sharp, and Arthur wasn't worried until it was too late."

"What is it?" Holly asked. "I recognize that look on your face. You've figured something out."

I brought my hand to my chest. "The spots on Arthur's sweater. The ones that glowed in the ultraviolet light."

"Speaking of lights," Julia said, tapping on her window. "The lights in that wretched hotel just went out again."

I twisted back to look out my passenger side window. "There's nothing wrong with those lights. That was done deliberately."

"Yes it was," Holly breathed.

"What if more than one of them is a murderer?" I said.

"What if they come out here?" Julia said. "We're defenseless."

"There's a shovel in the cargo area," Holly said, checking the door locks.

"Can you really see me hitting someone with a shovel?" Julia said.

"As a matter of fact, I can, yes," Holly said. "What's taking Chief Gilroy so long?"

"He thinks we drove home," I said. "He doesn't know we're trapped up here. Try your radio. It might work."

Holly punched a button on the dash. "How can that be?" she asked in amazement as music burst forth.

"They didn't take the radio fuse, I guess," I said. "Modern cars are a mass of relays and fuses. I thought it might work when I saw the dashboard light up. Can you turn to Shane's station?"

Holly pushed another button.

"We seem to have lost contact once more with the Grandview Hotel," a host was saying. "For the second night in a row. I'm telling you, people, they say there are no ghosts, but there's something unnatural going on in the foothills above Juniper Grove. Someone—or something—doesn't want us to broadcast."

"Claptrap," Julia said.

"We'll keep trying," the host went on, "but in the meantime, we have someone in the studio who may be able to shed light on the Grandview's haunted past. Raymond Jago, the brother of Arthur Jago, who died tragically and inexplicably yesterday."

"It wasn't inexplicable, it was murder," I shouted at the radio.

"Welcome, Raymond. You have our deepest condolences. Let me start by asking you this: Have you ever seen a ghost at the Grandview?"

"Oh, yes, yes," Raymond replied. "Last year—and not for the first time. And I'm not the only one who's seen them. Many guests have. Guests from all over the world. It's almost expected that if you stay at the Grandview, you'll experience the paranormal. For some it's exciting, for others it's a little too much. Unfortunately, my brother may have been a victim of the paranormal, one way or another."

"He's trying to profit from his brother's death," Julia said, her voice filled with revulsion.

"Sadly, the hotel has two unexplained murders now," the host continued. "I understand a TV show is interested in broadcasting live from the Grandview. *America's Most*

Haunted Hotels will be setting up shop in February, and they'll be bringing some pretty advanced equipment with them to detect paranormal activity. Thermographic cameras, infrared thermometers, night-vision cameras, and so on. The show has a reputation for finding ghosts if they're there."

"That's correct," Raymond said. "The show has an excellent track record of documenting the ghost phenomenon. And I'd like to extend an invitation to this radio station, which has been at the forefront of work at the Grandview, to join the TV folks in February."

"What bunk," Julia said.

"That's a generous offer, and I can tell you now, we will accept," the host said, growing deferential at the thought of the increased ad revenue.

"They're conveniently leaving out the fact that Raymond owns half the station," I said. As I listened to the two men talk, I angled my head for a better look at all three floors of the Grandview. There wasn't a single light in any window. Where were the crew's flashlights? I was beginning to fear for Shane's safety and growing more frustrated by the minute that I couldn't enter the hotel, question a suspect, or even examine my corkboard for clues I might have missed.

Most of all, I needed to ask Gilroy about the crime-scene report for Arthur's murder. Had blood been found between the doorframe and hinge side of the library door? Would he tell me if it had? He *was* angry with me, and honestly, I couldn't blame him. Instead of keeping Juniper Grove safe tonight, he was on his way to the Grandview. He didn't know it, but he was about to rescue me and my friends from ourselves again.

I recalled Gilroy scanning Arthur's sweater with the ultraviolet flashlight, and Holly explaining how honey and maple syrup glowed under ultraviolet. The bear claws and the honey-cinnamon rolls, she'd said, were the only pastries that would glow like that.

Conyer had devoured one roll after another. But then Shane had eaten bear claws, and I thought I remembered Dustin doing the same. Maria had given in to the call of pastries and eaten a chocolate croissant, but Holly's croissants didn't contain honey or maple syrup. Then again, maybe Maria's virtuous eating habits were for show only and she had eaten a bear claw while the lights were out.

My gaze dropped from the third floor to the hotel's door. Someone was pushing it open, stumbling out.

"That's Maria," I said. "What's wrong with her?"

Her mouth wide, her hands stretched out as though she were racing ahead, desperate to cling to the invisible thing that lay before her, Maria staggered toward Holly's SUV.

I popped open my door and ran to her. She collapsed on her side in front of me and clutched wildly at her back.

"Maria, what happened?" I said.

"Knife, knife," she repeated beseechingly.

I felt the knife in her back and pulled my hand away. "Who did this?"

"I don't know!" she cried. "It's dark. I didn't see. Why?"

Holly and Julia were at my side, doing their best to comfort Maria.

"Chief Gilroy we'll be here any second," I said. "I'm going to call an ambulance from the hotel."

"The phones," Maria closed her eyes. "The phones are out again. Why? Who's doing this? I'm scared."

"Don't move her," I instructed, taking off my coat and wrapping it about her, trying to avoid touching the knife and thereby doing more damage. Holly removed her scarf, folded it, and carefully set it under Maria's head.

In the dark I couldn't judge where the blade had entered and if it had struck anything vital, but Maria was still breathing, though shallowly, and I knew from research for my mystery novels that knife wounds ranged from the instantly fatal to the relatively minor—those that left the victim with nothing more than a few stitches.

In the pitch black of the hotel, Maria's attacker couldn't have been sure of a precise strike, and I prayed that imprecision would save her life.

"Headlights," Holly said, pointing off to her left. "It's Gilroy."

CHAPTER 16

With the hotel phones out and the police cruiser's radio and cell phones out of range, we had to risk moving Maria. Gilroy told Underhill to put her, along with the three of us, in his cruiser and head out of the foothills. As soon as his radio could make contact, he was to call an ambulance and wait for it.

Julia sat in the front of the cruiser, and Holly and I perched on the edge of the back seat, holding Maria as still as possible on the drive to Juniper Hills. She lay on her side, her stomach pressed to the back of the seat, the knife facing outward. Every fifteen seconds I checked to see that she was still breathing, and every fifteen seconds, miraculously, she was.

I'd hated watching Gilroy enter the Grandview by himself, hobbling in his fracture boot, especially now that he was without the cruiser or Underhill as backup, but there was no other solution. Maria needed medical attention, and Gilroy had ordered Holly, Julia, and I to leave.

Near the base of the foothills road, Underhill slowed gently, stopped, and tried his radio. He made contact.

The ambulance arrived in ten minutes—a short time that felt like an eternity. We all got out of the cruiser while the paramedics transferred Maria, who thankfully was still conscious. I said a prayer for her, we all got back into the cruiser, and I turned to Underhill. "Drop us off at the head of Finch Hill Road, and then go back to the Grandview, please. Gilroy needs your help."

"I'll drop you off at your house," he said.

"But we can walk from there. It's not far."

"Funny thing is, Rachel," Underhill said as he started the car, "the Chief is my boss, so I tend to follow *his* orders."

I sat back and bit my tongue.

Julia, on the other hand, began to nervously speculate out loud. "Who would stab Maria? What's she got to do with anything? They must have sneaked up on her in the dark. Did you hear what she said? She didn't have a clue who did it. And I bet Shane doesn't even know it happened. They're all probably looking for her right now."

Five long minutes later, Underhill let us out in front of my house. Judging by the way he sped off, his tires spinning on the slick street before gaining traction, he too was aware of the danger Gilroy was in.

"Gilroy will be fine," Holly said. "You know he can handle himself. How about that cocoa you were going to make?"

"Isn't it getting close to a baker's bedtime?" I replied.

"I can't sleep until I hear what's going on at the hotel and find out how Maria is. Besides," she added, heading through my front gate, "we have some crime solving to do."

"I'm sorry about your car," I said. "We'll send a tow truck in the morning."

"Believe me, Rachel, it's the least of my worries."

We slung our coats over kitchen chairs, and minutes later we were in my living room, sipping hot cocoa. Feeling a chill in the air, I'd turned the heat up. I was too fidgety to play with newspapers and kindling in the fireplace. If Conyer and Shane—and maybe even Ian—were in on Arthur's murder, Gilroy wouldn't stand a chance. Especially wearing his ankle boot. *That's ridiculous*, I thought, taking a deep, calming breath. *They're not all in it together.* "Underhill must be at the hotel by now," I said, checking my watch.

"I'm sure he is," Julia said, "and I'm sure Gilroy is fine."

I wasn't so certain. The events of last December, when he could have died after being driven off the road, or frozen to death in any icy canyon outside Juniper Grove, had disabused me of the idea that he was untouchable. Some kind of super cop who could never be hurt. When he was released from the hospital, he made sure I understood the nature of his job—how dangerous it was—before we continued our relationship. He gave me an out: I could leave before we became so entangled it was impossible for me to leave. But it was already too late. I'd fallen in love with him.

Still, most of the time I was proud that he was a police chief. His was a good job, a noble job. Though he'd only been hired by our little town because the city of Fort Collins, off to the east, didn't care for his unbending honesty. Gilroy was a straight arrow, and before coming to Juniper Grove, he had paid dearly for it. When he caught the mayor's wife driving drunk—and not for the first time—he had refused to buckle to pressure from the mayor and his cronies to let her go. Soon after the incident, he was searching for a new job. Luckily for me, he found Juniper Grove.

"I say Connie and Ian are back on the suspect list," Holly said. "I don't see Shane or the rest of his crew attacking Maria."

"But murder victims almost always know their

134

attackers," I said, "and I don't think Connie and Ian know Maria. They know Shane and Dustin because those two have done remotes from the hotel before, but Conyer and Maria are new to it."

We sat in silence for a while, sipping our cocoa, trying in our own ways to make sense of what few clues we had.

It was Julia who finally spoke. "I still don't understand what Herbert Purdy's death has to do with it all."

At first I'd thought there had to be a direct link between Arthur's murder and Purdy's death, an undiscovered connection between the two men, but no more. It wasn't about them, it was about money, and the only connection between the two men was that the killer had cleverly used Purdy's death to draw Arthur to his own.

"Purdy is a gravy train," I said. "The last I heard on the radio, Raymond Jago was raving about special ghost tours he planned for the Grandview. Ghost guest packages, Halloween weekends, more radio shows and TV shows. He had it all planned, and Arthur's death was a bonus. There are now two mysterious murders to advertise."

"I wonder what Arthur would have thought of Raymond's plans," Julia said.

"Didn't Connie tell us she was making headway talking Arthur into upgrading the Grandview?" Holly said. "That was her word. Headway."

"But right now they're doing too much business with the ghost crowd," Julia said. "She said that too."

"It sounds like Arthur may have been willing to drop the whole Purdy business and turn the Grandview into a proper hotel," I said. "Maybe not right away, but soon."

Holly sat forward and restlessly clinked her fingernails on her cup. "Raymond wouldn't have liked that. Those two brothers were at odds when it came to the future of the Grandview."

"But Raymond wasn't at the hotel when Arthur was killed," I said. "Though it was Raymond who introduced Shane to Arthur, and Raymond who first suggested a remote broadcast on the anniversary of Purdy's death."

"Really?"

"Connie told me."

Unable to sit still any longer, I set down my cup and walked to the window overlooking my front yard. I felt a chill from the windows. Mine seemed to be as leaky as the Grandview's. No wonder I was always turning up the heat or starting a fire. January was the coldest and deadest of months. By January, autumn had long since departed and spring was no more than a distant hope. Yet in its own way, the month was supremely beautiful, wiping away the old slate and preparing the world for the new. Snow blanketed my yard, wrapped itself around the remains of my rose bushes, and turned to icicles on my overburdened gutters, but beneath that protective layer of snow, a thousand roots and buds stood ready for the longer, sunnier days of March.

"They all had the opportunity to kill Arthur," I said, continuing to gaze out my window. "Any one of them could have. They all separated from each other at some point, and Arthur could have been murdered in as little as sixty seconds. But we don't need opportunity, we need motive." I twisted back from the window. "And that's what we haven't got."

"Then let's get it," Julia said. "You think it has to do with money, so let's start there."

"Who doesn't need more money?" Holly asked grimly.

I walked back to couch and sat, but my anxiety over

Gilroy and the shock of seeing Maria with a knife in her back—still very fresh in my mind—had left me unsettled and unable to relax or even lean back in my seat. "Who among them had the motive to kill Arthur and try to kill Maria?"

"Could Maria have stumbled upon something?" Julia asked.

"Like what?"

She shrugged. "I don't know. Connie and Ian digging up another fireplace? Or maybe she saw something the night Arthur died and talked about it to the wrong person."

"That's possible," Holly said. "It's also possible that someone up there is a raving lunatic who doesn't need a motive to kill people."

I reflexively checked my watch—for the third time since sitting down with my cocoa.

"I didn't mean that, and you know he's fine," Holly said.

"No, I don't, Holly. That's the problem. For goodness' sake, he has a broken ankle."

"He's getting along very well on it," Julia said. "It'll be off in two weeks."

"Underhill's a good cop too," Holly said.

"I know he is. But that hotel," I moaned. "Pitch black and full of lunatics."

"That's how I felt about my house when the power went out a year ago," Holly said.

Julia laughed.

"My in-laws were over. You weren't here then, Rachel. Remember, Julia? They were visiting from Omaha, and I was in the middle of cooking my first dinner for them in two years. My mother-in-law kept saying we should order pizza because even if the power came back on in a few minutes, dinner was bound to be ruined, and my father-in-law got it into his head that if the power came back on, a power surge could start a fire in the house. He floundered around in the dark, unplugging everything. He even went into our bathroom and unplugged the electric toothbrush. We had cords hanging everywhere."

"Sounds like a nightmare," I said. I knew what my friend was doing, of course. Distracting me with a domestic horror story. And I loved her for it.

"They haven't been back to the house," she said with a laugh. "We put them up at the Lilac Lane B&B when they come. Lord help the owners of that place if they ever have a power outage. I wouldn't put it past my in-laws to pull every electrical cord in the entire building."

I had just leaned back in my seat when my cell rang. I bolted to the kitchen, followed there by Holly and Julia, and pulled my phone from my coat pocket. "It's Gilroy," I said, looking at the screen.

He wanted me to know he was okay, and so was Underhill. The lights had gone out at the Grandview because someone had deliberately turned off the main circuit breaker. And the phones were out because the line had been cut.

Turner was on his way up, he said. As soon as he got there, they were all heading back to the station—the Swansons as well as all the radio people. He had "suggested"—in an I'm-serious police-chief voice, I was sure—that the Swansons close down the Grandview until it was safe to reopen it.

Underhill had contacted the hospital and found that Maria was expected to live. She'd been lucky, they said. Soft-tissue damage, but nothing she couldn't recover quickly

138

from.

Shane and his crew hadn't even realized that Maria was missing. Or so they had said.

CHAPTER 17

I made more hot cocoa and filled a large Thermos with it, determined to take it downtown to the police station. Bearing a hot beverage on a cold January night, one could show up at almost any inopportune time and be forgiven. That was my theory, anyway.

Julia, who never missed a chance to see Gilroy, came with me, but Holly headed home. If she was lucky, she'd get seven hours' sleep before having to rise and go to work again. I told her I would be at the bakery first thing tomorrow morning and fill her in on all the details. She yawned, gave a weary wave, and gingerly made her way across our unplowed street to her house.

While opening the door to my little shed-like garage, I slid on an icy patch of snow, my first warning that the day's melting snow had frozen over and made the streets touchy if not treacherous. "Slow and steady," Julia said as I drove for the station. "We survived the Grandview, so let's not ruin things by dying on the streets of Juniper Grove."

I pointed out that I was going about twenty miles an hour and death, at that speed, was unlikely.

The usual five-minute drive to the station took about eight, but to Julia's relief, we arrived safely and managed to find a parking spot directly in front of the building. Travis

Turner, the new officer, was at the front desk when we entered.

"Rachel," he said, grinning broadly, "it's been a while."

"That's right. I haven't seen you since—"

"The chief got forced off the road and went down the canyon."

"And tried to climb up it with a broken ankle."

"Oh, what an awful night," Julia chimed in.

I looked to my left to see Underhill ushering Shane into the lobby. They headed straight for the coffeemaker. "Tonight, you mean, Miss Julia?" Shane said. "Yeah, it's awful. Maria in the hospital, another failed broadcast, I can't go home *or* to the Grandview, and here we are, suspects of the Juniper Grove police."

"It could be worse," Julia said.

Shane came to a halt. "I'd love to hear how."

"You could be in Denver."

Shane's laughter echoed in the lobby. "You have a point. A small one, but a point."

"What are you doing here, Rachel?" Underhill asked. "Not that you're not welcome."

"Technically, I'm meddling." I raised my Thermos. "But I brought hot cocoa. Less caffeine than coffee."

"I don't suppose I could have some."

"Absolutely," I said. I took a Styrofoam cup from a stack by the coffeemaker and poured Underhill a short cup. I needed to reserve some for Turner, Shane, and Gilroy. "Has the library crime-scene report or autopsy on Arthur come back yet?"

"The autopsy did," Underhill said. "Nothing surprising there. He died from the stab wound. The weapon was a knife

141

from the hotel's kitchen, but then the Swansons told us it was missing. Now they probably have another one missing."

"The one used to attack Maria?"

"I'm guessing it was also taken from the hotel. We should have the report on the library crime scene any time now. The lab said they'd email a pdf tonight."

"Did they search for blood that had been cleaned up? I've read you can't see it under ultraviolet without spraying it with luminol first."

Underhill smiled. "That's right. Blood reacts with the luminol and glows blue under ultraviolet. Are you working on your next mystery?"

"Something like that." I turned to Shane. "Cocoa?" I asked.

"Yes, ma'am," he said, holding out a cup.

Underhill knew I wanted to talk to Shane—I could see it in his eyes. I poured another cup of cocoa, handed it to him, and asked him to take it to Gilroy. Underhill told Turner to keep an eye on Shane while he headed back to the interview room.

"Don't you worry, Officer," Shane said, taking a seat near mine. "I have no intention of becoming a fugitive. I can't wait to talk about this on my show, and how can I do that if I'm on the lam?"

Underhill rolled his eyes and headed back down the hall, and I poured another short cup, this one for Travis.

"Shane, if you had to guess, why was Arthur killed?" I asked. In my peripheral vision, I saw Turner watch us over the rim of his cup.

He didn't waffle for a second. "The hotel, I'm sure. Imagine what it and the land it sits on is worth."

"But no one who was at the hotel when Arthur was

killed stood to gain from his death."

"You're still convinced one of my crew killed him."

"And attacked Maria."

"Then maybe I'm wrong and Arthur wasn't killed because of the hotel. It might have been personal."

"Arthur seemed like a nice man no one would want to hurt," Julia said.

"It seemed that way to me," Shane said.

"Could it have to do with the radio station?" I asked.

"Nah. How could it?"

I poured Julia a cup of cocoa, and for the umpteenth time, I tried to sort out my thoughts on Arthur's murder. What should have made it easier to solve—the limited time window in which it could have occurred—was no help. It didn't limit the suspects much. Conyer headed to the basement first, I recalled, followed by Maria—after she was handed a flashlight. Then Dustin and Shane took off. Soon after, Holly and I went to the basement, and Arthur left to meet someone in the library. At some point Dustin and Shane became separated, because Shane was on his own when I saw him in the basement.

Then there were those curious glow-in-the-dark spots on Arthur's sweater. "No report on what the spots were on Arthur Jago's sweater?" I asked Turner.

"Nothing yet," he answered.

"What spots?" Shane said.

"Oh yes, you and Holly were talking about that in the car," Julia said.

I clammed up, pretty sure I shouldn't have mentioned a crime-scene detail like that. Not before Gilroy did. The best way to divert Shane from his question was to ask him a rather annoying one of my own. "Shane, I need to ask you again if you can think of any reason Dustin or Conyer would kill Arthur and hurt Maria. They can't hear you, so be completely honest."

The expression on his face was equal parts bewilderment and frustration. "Rachel, I don't know them well outside of work. I know Dustin more than Conyer, but still, we're colleagues, not best friends, and if they don't want to talk about their personal lives, I can't make them."

I nodded absentmindedly. *Bear claws and honey-cinnamon rolls.* Holly had said those were the only two pastries she'd brought whose ingredients could glow under ultraviolet light. But what about something else that might glow? Something from the kitchen or the guest rooms? Hand lotions, shampoos, tonic water?

I knew from plotting my mystery novels that certain bodily fluids glowed, like blood or even sweat. If the killer had wiped his anxious, sweaty forehead just before pushing Arthur into the knife . . .

"Are they doing a DNA test on those spots?" I asked Turner.

"Probably."

"Rachel, what spots are you talking about?" Shane said.

Pulling my phone from my coat pocket, I did a quick search on food ingredients and other materials that glow under ultraviolet light—a surprisingly extensive list. But one item in particular caught my eye.

"Mind if I have more cocoa?" Underhill said as he walked back into the lobby. "It has the perfect amount of caffeine. Keeps me awake without making me all jumpy."

"Go right ahead," I said, handing him the Thermos. "Please take more to Chief Gilroy too."

144

As Underhill turned to leave, I called to him. He stopped in his tracks and pivoted back. "Yup?"

"I wanted to ask you about Maria. You talked to the hospital about her?"

"Sure did. She's one lucky lady. When I called, the nurse said she was sitting up in bed. Kind of pasty looking after that shock, probably, but doing well. They're releasing her tomorrow morning."

I think my jaw hit the floor. "Tomorrow morning?"

"They said if she had come in earlier in the day, they would have released her tonight. Like I said, lucky."

"Or careful and precise," I said.

Underhill frowned. "That's the same word the chief used. *Precise*. What am I missing?"

"Arthur's wound was precise too, but in a different way," I said, thinking aloud.

"And here I thought that girl was dying in front of us," Julia said. "We couldn't get her to the hospital fast enough. She moaned and groaned, and I was sure she was unconscious part of the time."

"Shane, did you hear Maria scream or call out in any way when she was stabbed?" I asked.

"Like I kept telling the chief, none of us heard a thing. It's not like she screamed and we ignored her. She was in 108, said she had to use the restroom in her room, and two minutes later, the lights went out. Next thing I knew, the chief was telling me she was attacked."

Staring down at my phone's screen, I rose from my seat. Unbelievable. It was all coming together. Falling into place like pieces of a puzzle. "Why does your crew call Maria 'Miss Vitamin'?"

"Because she gobbles vitamins all day long," he said

145

with a chuckle. "Not cheap ones, specialty ones. Powdered vitamins in gel caps. She tells me they work better than tablets. No, let me restate that. She doesn't tell me, she *lectures* me."

"Do you know if she takes powdered vitamin B?" I said.

"B is her favorite," Shane said. "She's says B12 is the king of vitamins."

"What is it, Rachel?" Julia asked.

Before I could answer, Gilroy strode into the lobby, heading for the computer on the front desk. "Turner, check the email. The lab texted that they sent the report."

"Want more cocoa?" Underhill asked him, giving the Thermos a jiggle.

"No," Gilroy said. He shot me a puzzled look, though Underhill must have told him Julia and I were in the lobby. Maybe what puzzled him was the expression on my face. The one I was sure said, *I think I figured it out*. He gave me a single nod.

I walked to where he stood and held up my phone. "They call Maria Miss Vitamin because she takes so many. Her favorite vitamin is B."

"Here's the report, Chief," Turner said, clicking on an email.

Gilroy took my phone, read the screen, and then glanced at the computer screen. "Let me sit," he said to Turner.

A minute later, Gilroy told Underhill to drive to the hospital and place Maria Hall under arrest for the murder of Arthur Jago. Underhill, though clearly astonished by the order, drained the last of his cocoa, set the Thermos down, and dashed out the door.

"Wait a minute," Shane said. "She was stabbed in the back. Shouldn't you be arresting her attacker?"

I kept my mouth shut. Gilroy had figured it out before I had, and I wasn't going to step on his toes.

"She stabbed herself, Mr. Rooney," Gilroy said. "Very carefully."

Shane raised a quizzical eyebrow. "That's a nifty trick. I'd like to know how she did that."

"She put a knife in the hinge of a door and carefully backed into it," Gilroy said. "Making sure to avoid anything vital."

Shane looked from Gilroy to me. "You mean she did a Herbert Purdy?"

"She probably took a knife to the laundry room, just off the kitchen," Gilroy said. "The main circuit breaker is there. She positioned herself just right, backed into the knife, and then pulled the circuit breaker. That's my guess, anyway. I'm sure we'll find out. It might have been the perfect alibi—or temporary diversion—if not for Purdy."

Shane was rubbing his jaw like mad, trying to process what Gilroy was saying. "She said she had to go to her room. We didn't hear a thing after that."

"It's the same way she stabbed Arthur Jago," Gilroy said. "Only in his case, she was showing him how Herbert Purdy died. She positioned him and then shoved him, making sure she *didn't* avoid anything vital. He pulled away from the door and she helped him to the chair. He was in shock and didn't fight her—not that anyone would have heard him. At the time, only Mrs. Foster was on the first floor."

Julia's hand flew to her mouth.

"Maria killed Arthur?" Shane said. "That poor guy. He

147

never hurt a soul."

"The spots on Mr. Jago's sweater turned out to be trace amounts of vitamin B, which glows under ultraviolet light," Gilroy added.

"*Those* spots," Shane said.

"Isn't that something?" Julia said. "Who would know that?"

Gilroy smiled and gave me back my phone. "Someone who looks things up on the Internet."

"I thought . . . I never," Shane sputtered.

He was having a hard time reconciling what he was hearing with the Maria he knew. I couldn't blame him. I'd known her just two days and she didn't seem the murdering kind to me. How wrong our first, and second, impressions could be. "When Holly and I found Maria in the basement, she was shaking," I told him. "But I realize now she wasn't afraid. She'd just killed a man. Even someone with a cold heart might shake after that."

"The crime was planned, but the timing wasn't," Gilroy said. "She knew what to do, but she had to bide her time and wait for the right moment to do it."

"You mean when everyone separated," Shane said. "That explains why she didn't go with Conyer to the basement. I remember she demanded a flashlight, and I think . . ." He lifted his head and stared at the ceiling. "I think the library door was closed or almost closed when I walked by. That must have been when she did it. Fast and ruthless."

"I think she had a discreet talk with Arthur earlier in the day," I said. "'Meet me in the library, and I'll show you how I solved the Purdy puzzle.' Something like that."

Gilroy nodded. "Or she told him to give the photo album another look and see if he could solve it himself."

148

"That would have appealed to Arthur," Shane said. "Those photos were the first new evidence for public eyes in fifty years. I bet he was flipping through the album when Maria entered."

"And to confuse things, Maria put it back on the shelf and laid a recipe book on Arthur's lap," I said. "But she left traces of vitamin B on the album."

Julia shivered slightly and rose from her seat. "I don't know about anyone else, but I've had enough of murders at the Grandview Hotel. Rachel, would you mind driving me home?"

"You got it."

"You're free to go, Mr. Rooney," Gilroy said. "The Swansons and your crew, too. But don't go back to the hotel. Spend the night at the Lilac Lane B&B. I'll drive you. We still have to locate and process the new crime scene Miss Hall created."

CHAPTER 18

Julia and I stood at the back of the bakery, taking in the warm, delicious air, waiting for the morning crush to thin out. Holly looked tired but happy. Her bakery needed the business, and for some reason, business was going wild. I'd never seen so many people at the counter, even on Christmas Eve, her biggest day.

"I don't know how Holly and Peter can keep up with this," I said to Julia. "They're short their triple-deck oven, and they will be until next week."

"At times like this, they need to close their eyes, cross their fingers, and just buy it," Julia said. "Waiting until next week won't help them."

"They have to wait until a credit card payment shows up. You know how that is."

"Well, I guess being too busy for your number of ovens is not a bad problem to have," Julia said.

The bakery door opened again, letting in a blast of cold air. I wrapped my scarf tightly about my neck and looked toward the door. "Shane and Dustin," I said, tapping Julia on the arm.

"How lovely of them to visit. I bet they know how disappointed Holly was in the broadcasts. She was cheated out of her big chance."

"Shane honestly tried to help her. I have to give him that." When Shane looked my way I raised my chin, calling him over.

"Well, Rachel and Miss Julia, fancy meeting you two ladies here," he said after threading his way to the back.

"It's our home away from home," I said. "Mine, anyway."

"I don't blame you one bit. Not after tasting your friend's pastries. I'd set up my office in here."

Dustin, whose hair was still riding high, said, "Good morning, everyone" in a gravelly voice and edged his way to the counter. I figured he was still smarting over news of Maria. Or maybe he was exhausted. With dark rings under his eyes and puffy skin, he looked it. He and the rest of the crew had spent the night at the Lilac Lane B&B, which couldn't have been refreshing. Not after being hauled to the police station and questioned. Shane seemed fresh enough, but I'd learned that the man possessed an endless well of energy.

"I can't believe how crowded this place is this morning," I said.

Shane grinned and stared ahead. "Smell that yeast and sugar. What could be better than that on a frosty January morning?"

"Are you heading back to Fort Collins?"

"With a box full of donuts and bear claws."

"Where's Conyer?"

"Sleeping in the car. We couldn't budge him, even with the promise of cinnamon-honey rolls." Still grinning, he looked my way. More than energetic, the man was boundlessly cheerful. He reminded me of Holly, when her life wasn't crashing in around her.

I recalled the morning after Arthur died, when I watched Shane talk with Gilroy, Dustin and Maria chat, and Conyer play solitaire. I thought, *Find the motive and I'll find the killer*. But it wasn't the motive that had led us to Maria. And in any case, I'd misjudged the motive, thinking it had to do with the hotel or the money it might bring.

Motive was paramount in my mystery novels, but with Arthur's murder, the clear, hard clues had pointed an unmistakable finger in the total absence of motive. It wasn't until Gilroy talked to Maria and later called me at home that I knew *why* she had murdered Arthur.

"I'm sorry about Maria," I said. "I didn't get a chance to tell you that at the station."

Shane stuffed his hands in his coat pockets. "Yeah, well, it's Arthur I feel sorry for. He trusted her."

"Anyone would have. She's a small woman, innocent looking, never been to the hotel before."

It turned out that Maria hadn't realized that Arthur owned the Grandview until she read up on the Purdy mystery in preparation for the radio show. She *had* read Shane's folder—she had studied it, in fact—and she had begun to suspect that Purdy died at his own hands. Even if he hadn't, what a great way to kill someone, she'd thought. Perfect for revenge. And considering Arthur's interest in Purdy, what wonderful irony.

Seventeen years earlier, when Maria was a teenager, her father had been fired from his job as CEO of a company run by Arthur Jago. He was an alcoholic who was ruining the business, but that didn't figure into Maria's teenage thinking. Her father never found another job, he never recovered from the disgrace of being fired, and he took his own life a year later.

From her hospital bed, and with vengeful glee, Maria told Gilroy that Arthur had wondered why she was wearing gloves when she set the knife between the door and frame. He thought she was cold, and he offered to turn up the heat. She also admitted to vandalizing Holly's car after hearing her drive up on the second night. It was just one more way to confuse the investigation—and easier than injuring herself with a kitchen knife.

"In a way, Arthur solved the Purdy mystery," Julia said. "After fifty years. He'd be happy about that."

"You make me laugh, Miss Julia," Shane said.

"Do I?" Julia said, looking pleased with herself.

"We'll have to meet again," he said.

"Well, I would like that very much."

"But for now . . ." He took his hands out of his pockets. "It was a pleasure to meet you both. Rachel, you keep up with the keen observations, and Miss Julia, you keep being an optimist. The world needs more of them. I have to get in there and get our pastries. We've got a meeting at the station in an hour." He nodded a farewell and maneuvered his way through the crowd until he stood next to Dustin.

"What a nice young man," Julia said. "So much nicer than I ever imagined he would be." She nudged me with her elbow. "And look who just walked in."

A nudge from Julia could mean only one thing: Gilroy. When he saw me, he smiled, swung around the back of the crowd, and weaved his way to where we stood.

"Chief Gilroy, how lovely to see you this morning," Julia gushed.

"Mrs. Foster, good morning."

"You have a wait ahead of you," I told him, slipping my arm into his.

"I see."

"Are you going to talk to me about meddling?"

He kissed my cheek. "I worry about you. You run headlong into things."

"I know I do."

"Just tell me next time, okay? I mean *before* you go to a place like the Grandview."

"I will. I promise."

He looked at me skeptically, as though he didn't quite believe me. But I meant it. No more taking off without telling him. He was right—I could be rash. But my new resolve was based on more than the rather late-blooming self-awareness that I could act foolishly. It had been twelve years since a man had worried enough about me to say, *Tell me when you go somewhere. I mean it.* And even then that man, my ex-fiancé, hadn't really cared. He'd just wanted to keep tabs on me, something I became painfully aware of the day he walked out on me.

Gilroy didn't think I was frail or incompetent, and he wanted me to be free to pursue the things that mattered to me. He just worried when I dabbled in murder. Really worried. Like I worried when people shot at him or forced him and his cruiser down a steep canyon.

"Where did all these people come from?" I asked. "It's like half the town is here."

"I'm not surprised," he said. "Did you listen to the radio this morning?"

Gilroy told me he had driven Shane, Dustin, and Conyer back to the Grandview at six o'clock in the morning so they could load up their SUV and head home. Shane had asked one favor—a five-minute on-air talk with his station in town. The morning show would make time for him in, he

154

said.

"You let him?"

"I didn't think it could hurt," he said with a shrug. "We knew Maria hadn't stabbed herself in room 108. Rooney talked about what had happened last night, that Arthur Jago's killer had been caught, and said he'd say more about it when he got back to town. Then he spent the last two minutes telling everyone that the pastries at Holly's Sweets were the best he'd ever had, anywhere, and he planned to make a stop at the bakery before going home."

"Oh, he *is* a nice young man!" Julia said.

So that's why Shane had smiled enigmatically when I'd mentioned how crowded the bakery was. He knew *why* it was crowded. "Good for him."

"He said he'll mention the bakery this coming Monday too, during a special program on the solution to the Purdy ghost mystery. Apparently, it's already been planned."

"He'll have his largest audience ever," I said. "Holly and Peter won't be able to keep up." *Literally*, I thought. *Not with their big triple-decker out of commission.* Holly had said she was buying a new oven next week, but Shane's special was on Monday, four days away. She was going to need help.

"They need to hire temp help," Gilroy said.

"What they need is a new oven. Their big one bit the dust, and they can't afford a new one until after Shane's Monday show."

"So *that's* why the rush."

"What rush?"

"Look," he said, gesturing with his head at the counter.

After taking a large pastry box from Holly, Shane passed if off to Conyer and then handed her a few bills and a long brown envelope. Mouthing the word "What?" she turned the envelope over in her hands. Shane gave her the same cryptic grin he'd given me and walked with Dustin out of the bakery. Smiling all the way.

Holly put the cash in the register and stepped back from the counter just as Peter came around the corner with two trays of croissants. "One second," she said to a customer, holding up an index finger. "Just one second."

Peter scowled, his attention divided between the trays he was sliding into the display counter and the envelope Holly was tearing open.

She drew out a slip of paper. Her eyes narrowed. Then her jaw dropped.

She said something to her husband and, still staring at the paper, she came up behind him and grabbed his shoulder. He took the paper, and a moment later, his jaw dropped too.

"What is it?" I asked Gilroy.

"That should be a check from Raymond Jago. When I drove Rooney's crew up to the hotel, he asked me when the bank opened, and I guess it was a little late for him because he said he needed to contact a courier service immediately. I asked why, and he said Jago wanted to pay his brother's debt to Mrs. Kavanagh. And then he said something about a down payment for future events at the Grandview, whatever that means."

"Shane must have told Raymond Jago that Holly had missed out," Julia said. "I told you he was a nice man."

"I never said he wasn't, Julia. Turns out Raymond Jago's not too bad himself." I jostled my way to the front of the crowd and waved Holly to my place at the counter.

"Ten thousand dollars," Holly said, showing me the check for concrete proof. Her eyes were glistening with

156

tears. "It has to be wrong. We just brought pastries."

"You missed out on the advertising they promised you," I said. I felt a huge grin form on my face. "Raymond Jago can afford it. It's not wrong. It's just right. And you need to buy an oven immediately. Today. Shane plans to rave about your bakery again on Monday, and you have to be prepared."

She leaned across the counter and whispered, "Again? Did he talk about us? Is that why we're so busy?"

"Yup."

"Ma'am," a customer called impatiently.

"Go," I said, waving Holly off. "You've got new customers to impress."

I worked my way back to Julia and Gilroy—I was certain the crowd had grown in the past sixty seconds—and told them that Holly's worries about a new oven were over.

Julia, always one for specifics, asked if it was a large check.

"Very," I said. "Should we start moving forward? The crowd keeps getting ahead of us and I need my cream puffs."

"We can't lose our place," Gilroy replied, taking me by the arm.

Place. The very word made me smile again. Juniper Grove was my place. It held my friends and the man I'd been waiting for my whole life. Every once in a while, a fresh face—like Shane's—breezed into town and back out again, and if they were kind and good, I was glad to meet them. But I wasn't leaving. Not that I wouldn't take trips, of course, but I would always come *home*. And finally—I was so blessed in this—I knew where home was.

FROM THE AUTHOR

We all need a place to escape to from time to time. A place where neighbors drink cups of coffee around a kitchen table (and some indulge in cream puffs), where friends feel safe sharing their hearts' deepest yearnings, where neighbors stop to chat with neighbors outside flower shops. True, the occasional murder mars the Juniper Grove landscape, but what would a mystery series be without dead bodies? Juniper Grove is still that place of escape, and I hope you'll join me there for all the books in the series. I look forward to sharing more of Rachel Stowe and her friends with you.

If you enjoyed *Scared to Death*, please consider leaving a review on Amazon. Nothing fancy, just a couple sentences. Your help is appreciated more than I can say. Reviews make a huge difference in helping readers find the Juniper Grove Mystery Series and in allowing me to continue to write the series. Thank you!

KARIN'S MAILING LIST

For giveaways, exclusive content, and the latest news on the Juniper Grove Mystery Series and future Karin Kaufman books, sign up to the mail and newsletter list at KarinKaufman.com.

MORE BOOKS BY KARIN KAUFMAN

ANNA DENNING MYSTERY SERIES

The Witch Tree
Sparrow House
The Sacrifice
The Club
Bitter Roots
Anna Denning Mystery Series Box Set: Books 1-3

CHILDREN'S BOOKS (FOR CHILDREN AND ADULTS)

The Adventures of Geraldine Woolkins

OTHER BOOKS IN THE JUNIPER GROVE MYSTERY SERIES

Death of a Dead Man
Death of a Scavenger
At Death's Door
Death of a Santa
Scared to Death
Cheating Death
Death Trap

PREVIEW OF *CHEATING DEATH*
Juniper Grove Cozy Mystery Book 6

CHAPTER 1

I was on my way to my friend Holly Kavanagh's bakery when I first spotted Brigit Gundersen and her industrial-sized staple gun. She was making her way down Main Street at a furious pace, stapling flyers to tree trunks and anything else she could drive a staple through. When she reached Grove Coffee and its metal front door, she pulled a roll of duct tape from her purse, yanked out a foot-long stretch of it, and tore it from the roll with her teeth.

She glanced up and saw me half a block away, obviously watching her—I'd come to a full stop in the middle of the sidewalk—and acknowledged me with a slithery grin. Then she slapped a flyer to the cafe's door and secured it with the tape.

"Rachel Stowe," she called, heading my way. "Let me give you one of these."

Whatever she was going to show me, I wanted none of it. I smelled trouble. The kind that drags you in with claws and won't let you go. It was Wednesday, Valentine's Day was on Friday, and I had a boyfriend for the first time in twelve years. I was in a cheery mood, and Brigit was not going to ruin it.

Boyfriend. A strange word for a forty-three-year-old woman to use, and I smiled at the unexpected sweetness of it. Brigit thought I was smiling at her.

"You won't be smiley-faced when you see this." She thrust a flyer at me.

Beneath a photo of her husband was the word "Cheater" in bold red letters.

"And that's what he is," Brigit said. "Big time."

I was speechless.

"You didn't think Wayne was the cheating type, did you?" she said, dropping the duct tape into her purse. She smelled strongly of stale cigarettes and less strongly of alcohol. Whiskey, maybe, but I was no expert.

"I've never really thought about it," I said.

"That's because you always think the best of people, Rachel. Even men. Save yourself a lot of trouble and stop it."

"What happened, Brigit?"

"Just what the flyer says. Wayne is a cheater. Can you believe he admitted it? Twenty-one years of marriage and not an ounce of shame. You know how women say things like, 'I wasted the best years of my life on you'? Well, it's true. I'm forty-six, and I wasted my youth on him. I'll never get it back." She tottered slightly on her red high heels and steadied herself by grabbing my arm. "I don't even have kids anymore. They flew the coop. Or the nest, is it? I think it's the nest. Whatever it is, they're off. They're gone." She let go of me and tucked a strand of blonde hair behind her ear.

"I'm sorry." What else could I say? I barely knew the Gundersens. We'd first met in mid-December at Juniper Grove's annual spaghetti dinner for charity, and then in January I'd run into them at the bakery two or three times. That was it.

"He won't tell me who it is," she said through clenched teeth. "It's two days before Valentine's Day."

"I know."

"Rubbing salt in my wounds, that's what it is. It's deliberate. He knew I'd find out. He wanted me to."

"I'm sorry." I was a fount of wisdom.

"I could die. It's so humiliating."

Humiliation wasn't her concern. After all, she was advertising her husband's cheating ways up and down Main Street. "Do you think maybe . . . you know, the flyers. Maybe they're not a good idea."

"They're not an idea, they're a plan. And a very clever one."

"Maybe they're not the best plan."

"He won't tell me who it is," Brigit said, ignoring my fainthearted attempt to stop her from plastering more trees and shops. "I found lipstick. Dark hairs on his suits, too. He's been distant for a long time, but I ignored that. I should have known long ago. Do you know what I found when I came home early from—"

"Brigit, you shouldn't be telling me this. Talk to your husband, or a close friend."

"Or a lawyer."

"If you want."

She leaned in close, the alcohol on her breath more pungent. "I have to humiliate him like he humiliated me. First I called his boss at Mountain Real Estate, now I'm telling the rest of Juniper Grove." Taking tiny, careful steps in her not-for-drinking heels, she turned and looked back up the sidewalk, surveying her extensive handiwork. Two or three people stood at every flyer, reading, gaping in

163

wonderment, shaking their heads. "I've succeeded," Brigit said. "Wouldn't you say?"

That depends on what you mean by success. I bit my tongue. She looked back at me, expecting an answer.

"I taped one to the bakery door, too," she said. "You and Holly are friends, right?"

"Yes."

"She saw me taping it and didn't look too pleased. She's probably ripped it off by now." Her expression became thoughtful. "Wait. Holly has dark hair. And she's in her late thirties, right? Wayne would like that."

"Hold on, Brigit. Don't even start. Holly doesn't cheat on her husband." I wanted to quash Brigit's budding suspicion before it blossomed. Pain was causing Brigit to behave irrationally, and if she got it into her head that Wayne was having an affair with Holly—she had no idea how laughable the idea was—she'd start spreading rumors.

"Rachel, I'm only running through all the dark-haired women I know. Just making a list in my mind."

"Leave Holly off it."

Her eyes narrowed. "You have dark hair."

"Oh, for goodness' sake, Brigit."

"Though there's gray in it, and Wayne isn't into gray."

"Please call someone to take you home."

"My car's two blocks down. As soon as I finish." She waved the small stack of flyers.

"You drove here?"

She looked at me as though I were quite dense. "I live two miles outside of downtown. I'm supposed to walk?"

"Well, yes. Sometimes." Although I was growing more impatient by the minute, I forced myself to speak as gently as possible. "Like today. I don't think it's safe for you to drive. I'd be happy to drop you off at your house. It's no problem."

"So you can what? Come back here and warn Wayne about what I've done?"

"It's none of my business." Why was I trying to reason with her? The police station was half a block ahead. If she insisted on driving home in her inebriated state, I'd tell Chief Gilroy or Officer Underhill. I wasn't about to let her stumble off, putting herself and others in danger.

"It's everyone's business now," she said. "Wayne's little secret is a secret no more."

"What is this?" a man shouted. "Brigit!"

Brigit froze at the sound of her name. She wobbled around and looked up the sidewalk, where small crowds still gathered about her flyers.

She didn't have to worry about me warning Wayne— not that I'd intended to stick my nose in their messy business—because someone else had done the job. He was on the sidewalk near his real estate office, tearing flyers from every tree and storefront. As he shredded them in his shaking hands, his eyes shot daggers at her and he shouted her name.

Brigit smiled serenely.

A moment later, Officer Derek Underhill exited the police station, making his way to the source of the commotion. Brigit's smile exploded into a grin.

"Revenge," she breathed.

I'd had enough. I wrote mystery novels for a living— crafting plots about revenge and deceit—but seeing and hearing such raw emotion in the flesh made me queasy. After seven years as an editor in Boston, I'd returned to my home state of Colorado and found Juniper Grove, my little town nestled against the foothills of the Rockies, so I could enjoy the sweet life. And this was not sweet.

When I started for the bakery—I'd resolved to have a little talk with Underhill about Brigit's sobriety on the way—Brigit grabbed hold of my arm.

"Rachel, you can find out who Wayne's having an affair with. You're like a detective."

"I'm nothing like a detective. Talk to a lawyer, Brigit."

"Everyone in town knows you solve murders. A cheating husband should be a piece of cake."

"I can't get involved."

"I'll pay you. I just need to know who this woman is. Can you understand that? I have my suspicions, but I need to know for sure. I'll lose it if I don't. Is she who I think it is? Why does he love her and not me?"

My heart went out to her. Underneath the crazy anger was an anguished wife. "Brigit, I don't do things like this, and you need to talk to a lawyer."

Underhill, who had turned his attention to Brigit, was heading our way, so I left her behind, intercepted him, and quickly told him that she was in no shape to drive home. Thankfully, he understood immediately and assured me she wouldn't be getting into her car.

By the time I reached the bakery, my cheerful mood had evaporated. Even the sight of Holly's freshly baked cream puffs—the best pastries in Colorado—couldn't lift my sagging spirits. I waited at the back for two customers to leave and then strolled to the counter. "You saw Brigit Gundersen's flyer? She said she taped one to your door."

Holly wrinkled her nose. "I threw it away. I take it I'm not the only business she visited?"

"She's been up and down Main Street."

"Wait until Wayne finds out."

"He already has." I bent down for a better look at the cream puffs. One or two? That was the question. "He's out there now, ripping them up."

"If she's accusing him falsely, that's libel. Or is it slander?"

"She wrote it down, so I think it's libel. But Brigit says Wayne admitted he's been cheating." I straightened. "I'll take two cream puffs."

Holly grabbed a small pink box and placed two of her larger puffs in it. "Last year Brigit told me she was thinking about moving to Denver, and she never once mentioned Wayne. I just assumed they'd go together. All I could think was, why on earth would you move to Denver?"

"I can't imagine why." I dug into my jeans pocket and handed her a ten. *Why on earth, indeed*. Denver, only sixty miles to the southeast of Juniper Grove, was a different world, and the residents of our little town liked it that way. "What do you know about Brigit and Wayne as a couple?"

"They've been living in Juniper Grove about eight years. I think they've been married about twenty. They've never struck me as a happy couple, though I'm not sure why. It's just a feeling I have. In spite of how they act in public, they're not happy together." She handed me my change and propped her elbows on the counter. "Peter and I were invited to dinner at their place two years ago. They have a beautiful house on the east side of town. Wayne spent the whole evening picking on Brigit. Little things, mostly subtle, but it was pick, pick, pick, all night long. I kept expecting Brigit to explode, but she never did."

"Maybe she waited until her guests left."

"And then threw a cast-iron skillet at him."

The bakery door opened, ushering in a gust of cold wind along with Officer Underhill. "I got sidetracked by all the excitement," he said, grinning at me. "I meant to pick up donuts."

"Did Brigit get off safely?" I asked.

"Officer Turner's taking her home."

Holly shot me a questioning sidelong glance and grabbed another pink box. "Half a dozen assorted donuts, Officer?"

"You got it."

Despite what I'd told Brigit about not wanting to get involved, my growing concern for her, and my curiosity, were beginning to get the best of me. If anyone knew what was going on between the Gundersens, it was Underhill. Garrulous, indiscreet Underhill.

"I wonder if someone should check on Brigit later," I said, looking straight at the officer. "She's not thinking clearly, and Wayne was pretty angry."

"Those two should have divorced long ago," Underhill said. "Now that both their kids are out of the house and going to college out of state, they should call it a day. Save us all the misery."

"Has Brigit ever done anything like that before?"

"The flyers? No, that's a new one. But the Gundersens have fought in public before. I don't know why, but it doesn't bother them to air their dirty laundry in public. They provoke each other, you know? Wayne has a temper, and Brigit likes to push his buttons—and sometimes vice versa."

Holly slid Underhill's box across the counter. "Is Wayne violent?"

"Nah." Underhill's hand froze on the box. "I don't think so. Not that I know of."

"Is Brigit violent?" I asked.

Laughing merrily at my foolishness, Underhill paid for his donuts. "She's a hundred pounds and five foot four, Rachel. What could she do to Wayne?"

"Weapons are great equalizers," I replied.

Underhill's smile melted. I'd ruined his donut outing.